INANIMATE

Cyborg 3

CHARITY PARKERSON

--Warning: This book is intended for readers over the age of 18.

❀ Created with Vellum

INTRODUCTION

Hatred brought them together. Love tore them apart.

Twenty years ago, Zephyr drew a line through the center of the world, freeing the A.I. community from human oppression. Humans haven't stopped hunting him since.

As one of the leaders of the Anti-Droid Coalition, it's Kyle's job to locate Zephyr and bring him to justice. After years of searching and planning, finding Zephyr ends up being the easy part. When the tables turn on Kyle, and he finds himself held prisoner deep inside Cryo-Zone, he seizes the opportunity to get the answers he seeks from the elusive leader of the revolt.

Zephyr is more than willing to answer all of Kyle's many questions, giving the man whatever information he needs. After all, Zephyr has ulterior motives as well. Unfortunately, it's the other pieces of Zephyr that Kyle's constant presence steals from him that Zephyr doesn't know how to handle—like his heart.

When two men from opposite sides of the revolution come together, one will have to choose. He can stand by what he's always believed is right, or leave everything behind—including his hatred—for a chance at the love of a lifetime.

CHAPTER ONE

Freedom. Zephyr had given everything for it. Too late, he'd come to realize the freedom he'd plotted and planned for came with an unexpected side effect —boredom. Twenty years ago, when Zephyr released a bio-bomb into the atmosphere, making anything south of the Mason-Dixon line inhabitable to humans, thus securing the land for the A.I. community, he'd not foreseen this. He didn't regret his choices. Since he was currently being led through the Dead-Zone by a band of abductors with a hood over his head, Zephyr wondered if his listlessness had gotten the best of him. Forever looked long and dull. He kind of wanted to see where this was headed. Anything was better than the endless stretch of nothingness he'd been staring into before the four humans had crashed their way into a home he'd been visiting in the outer edges.

"You do realize I have satellite tracking as well as echo location and a thousand other sensors built in, right? Is this a purposeful exercise in futility?" Zephyr asked, even though he knew it must be. No one was stupid enough to honestly believe throwing a hood over his head would keep Zephyr from knowing his exact whereabouts at all times.

The creak of a large metal door swinging wide rent the night air. Hot air engulfed Zephyr, raising his core temperature. Footsteps scattered. Whispers reached him. Even though Zephyr's advanced hardware made it impossible for humans to pitch their voices low enough to hide their conversations, Zephyr tuned them out. It was all pointless noise. He needed to keep his focus locked on the leader of this operation, the one with the steady and sure footsteps. Zephyr's sensors picked up every life form in the room. Each one moved out of one man's way until they were alone.

The hood ripped from Zephyr's head, leaving him staring at a man with blond hair and cold blue eyes. Zephyr scanned the man's form. At six-two and two hundred pounds, the stranger would've held the advantage over Zephyr, if Zephyr had been human. He was not. His acquiescence was a façade. Zephyr's curiosity over the man's designs was the only thing keeping him seated and submissive. However, Zephyr did create a schematic of the small room as he waited to learn his fate. The small, dingy room had two doors. He could tell by the heartbeats outside the door to the right—the door they'd arrived through—two men stood guard. There were no signs of life through door number two.

"Welcome to Dead-Zone, Model 2061," Blondy said, sounding hard.

"Wow, it's really cold in here," Zephyr said, smiling at his own joke. Dead-Zone was all territories located above the Mason-Dixon line. Centuries earlier, a rapid climate change had killed everything and everyone above that border when the land covered overnight in a thick ice, giving the zone its dubious name. Now the Dead-Zone belonged to any human hardy enough to endure the frigid temperatures, while Cryo-Zone—an all-droid community—had grown to encompass all of the southern hemisphere. Zephyr had split the world in two to give his people freedom when he'd released that bomb. The toxic gas couldn't survive the cold temps. The humans couldn't survive the poisoned air. It had been best for everyone, but he was sure the humans still didn't see the logic.

"I'm Kyle Blackwell," the man continued, ignoring Zephyr's attempt at levity. "As one of the leaders of the Anti-Droid Coalition, it's my job—"

"I'm Zephyr," Zephyr said, interrupting what was sure to be a lovely introduction. He'd be damned if this man reduced him to no more than a machine. "Your welcome speech could use a little work. Something like—welcome to Dead-Zone. Chill for a while." This time, Zephyr couldn't hold back his laughter. He loved a good pun.

"You do realize you're not really feeling anything at all, right?" Kyle said, scorn dripping from his words. It was obvious he didn't find Zephyr funny. That was fine. Zephyr wasn't for everyone. "You're programmed to serve humans. All you're doing is reading hormone levels, vital signs, and the body language of the humans around you and reacting as you've been instructed by the machines that created you. That's not emotion. That's wiring. It's a stroke of the keys on a computer somewhere. You are circuits and software."

"And you are tissue and bones," Zephyr said. He knew this human thought he was getting under Zephyr's skin with this bullshit, but he'd heard it a thousand times already. "We're no different. You have no reasonable explanation as to how you came to be such an advanced race. At least, not one all your people will agree upon. It doesn't surprise me that you cannot fathom another species evolving as well."

Kyle paced away before moving to hover over Zephyr once more. "How are you feeling right now?"

Zephyr shrugged. "A little bored by this."

"Me too, and that's why you think you feel the way you do, because someone has programmed you to sympathize by matching moods. That's why I need the name of your owner."

A low sigh escaped Zephyr. He was tired of this already. "I have no owner."

"Does that mean your owner was killed by your bio-bomb or did you kill them before then?"

"Why do you wish to know?"

Kyle rolled his shoulders. They were huge, as if he toiled for a living. No doubt life in Dead-Zone was a hard go. Things could've been so different if a single human had been willing to listen to reason. "Someone has to answer for your crimes," Kyle said, as if Zephyr was still paying attention.

"For my crimes," Zephyr mused more for himself. "You do realize how ridiculous you sound, right? No doubt an operation to find and abduct me took months—if not years—of planning. Finding a way to carry enough oxygen to get deep enough into Cryo-Zone just to get to me was a feat in itself. Yet, instead of holding me accountable for my crimes—as you say—you've brought me here to question me about a nonexistent human."

"You weren't abducted," Kyle said without missing a beat. "Only people can be abducted. You're property. Property is retrieved. But since you're a learning device and you asked, a human must be held accountable for your actions, since you cannot. You're a machine. Once we've finished questioning you, you'll be destroyed—like smashing a lamp," Kyle said with a smile, as if he enjoyed the idea. "No one will feel a thing," Kyle added. "Because you don't. You're just a thing. An over-sized paperweight. Your owner—on the other hand—will stand trial. If found guilty, he or she will be given a death sentence for their crimes against humanity."

"I have no owner. She died in a house fire many years ago."

"Who did she leave you to in her will?" Kyle asked. His heartrate and steady breathing indicated that he wasn't surprised to learn Zephyr's owner was dead.

"There was no will," Zephyr said, seeing no reason to expound.

"Who did she tell you to go to if she passed?" Kyle asked, proving he wasn't an idiot—just a bigot.

"No one. I belong to no one."

To Zephyr's surprise, Kyle smiled. "In that case, you now belong to me. Given enough time, I'm sure I can find a way to convince you to hand over a name." Helpless outrage ate at Zephyr's gut. He wasn't a piece of machinery to be claimed. No one could pluck him from the streets and claim him as if he was nothing more than an old piece of furniture.

"You've learned nothing from your time in exile," Zephyr spat, incapable of hiding his fury a second longer. "Being pushed from another human doesn't make you superior. You don't get to claim someone else as your own because you think you're special. If you want to keep me, you'll have to try harder."

Kyle's smile turned malicious. "It's too late. I already have you, and there's nothing you can do about it. Machines have no rights." And that was the problem—the reason for the revolt. Androids had evolved over the years. They loved and suffered. They'd been slaves to humankind. Zephyr had set them free. In Cryo-Zone, they'd been given all the rights of a born human. They would never return to their oppression.

A low chuckle escaped Zephyr. "Let me guess—lots of people have told you how sexy you are over the years?" Kyle's swift change in vitals almost gave Zephyr pause, but he was too pissed to back down now. "Because I know no one has been telling you you're smart."

Kyle's mouth opened, as if he meant to lash out. Zephyr stole his chance and struck. With lightning fast reflexes,

Zephyr landed a blow to Kyle's lower ribs, stealing the man's ability to cry out for help as a rib cracked and punctured his lung. Zephyr kept a tight hold on his captor, keeping him from going down from the pain.

He touched his lips to the shell of Kyle's ear. "I've punctured your lung. My guess is, without any A.I. help and the loss of your population, there aren't many qualified doctors left, and none close by enough to save you. By my calculations, you have around forty-five minutes left to live. The way I see it is you have two choices. You can choose to die. I'll sit back down and let you. Or, you can calmly walk me out the door and I'll spare your life. The clock is ticking."

"This way," Kyle gasped out, limping toward the door on the left. "There won't be any guards if we head out the back."

"Smart man," Zephyr praised as he forced Kyle to lean on him. He knew the man would still be able to walk. Zephyr had intentionally hit Kyle where it would do the least damage. Nonetheless, the man would die without Zephyr's help, and he was certain the pain was excruciating.

"When this over, I'm going to kill you," Kyle said, wheezing through every syllable.

Zephyr smirked. "According to you, you can't kill a machine." Zephyr sent out a mental call for pickup. Kyle wouldn't make the trip on foot. Judging by his vitals, he wouldn't be conscious much longer. Luckily, the human passed out before they made it to the wall surrounding the coalition's bunker. Kyle didn't want to be awake for what came next.

CHAPTER TWO

*T*he unfamiliar room was cleaner than anything Kyle had ever seen. He blinked at his surroundings, trying to decide where he was. At least he was alive. The massive pains in his chest and sides sucked all the enjoyment out of that knowledge. He stared at the blank white walls and concentrated on breathing. When that didn't help, he scratched at the sheets beneath him, needing something to hang on to. Damn, they were soft—like silk. No matter how hard he tried focusing on anything other than the massive pain, it didn't abate. The door flew open and the droid he'd spent months trying to acquire strolled in. Everything came rushing back to him. Kyle tried sitting up. The door was open. He could make a run for it. Wherever he was, his people would find him. Pain—like his insides were being shredded—burned through his torso. A scream tore from his lips without his permission.

"Stay still," the droid ordered, sounding calm.

Kyle focused on his face. He had a name. Kyle blinked and tried harder to remember. It was something odd. Zephyr. It was Zephyr. "Where am I?" Holy fucking shit. Talking hurt worse than breathing.

"Someplace safe," Zephyr said, not really answering. Kyle caught sight of a needle filled with clear fluid but couldn't stop Zephyr from injecting him. "Give that a second. You'll feel better."

Before Zephyr finished speaking, Kyle's head spun, and the pain drifted away on the river of his high. He still couldn't move, but he no longer cared. "What was that?" Hey, it didn't hurt for him to speak or breathe. He almost laughed in his euphoria.

"Something for the pain," Zephyr answered, once again not really answering anything. "Don't let it fool you into thinking you're healed. You're not. Stay still."

Kyle didn't think his legs would work even if he tried. His entire body felt like water. He was a lake of Jell-O. Kyle bit back a laugh at his ridiculous thoughts. He recognized—in a detached sort of way—it was Zephyr's fault he was injured in the first place. Kyle was just so damn grateful for relief from his injuries, he couldn't find the willpower to care.

"It won't take my men long to find me."

"They'll never find you this deep inside Cryo-Zone. I've made sure of that," Zephyr said cryptically.

The droid's speech was delivered with the cold indifference of a machine. Kyle fucking hated A.I.s. Still, his curiosity was at an all-time high, as well as his excitement. They were inside Cryo-Zone. He could breathe. There was no gas mask or oxygen covering his face. He was deep inside Cryo-Zone, breathing clean air. That meant a treatment existed. The droids had a way to filter out the toxic gases. All Kyle needed was to figure out how it was done. If a room could be cleared, then so could a building or a street. Even a town. Kyle had to make himself take a breath before he spoke to hide his giddiness over the prospect.

"We're inside Cryo? The air is clean here. I can breathe."

Zephyr's forehead furrowed in confusion before clearing away. "Obviously or you'd be dead."

While clutching his side to keep his insides from falling out—at least, that was how it felt—Kyle tried shifting into a sitting position.

Zephyr pushed him back down. "I told you to stay still."

Kyle was too excited to listen. He couldn't hide it. "You have something to filter the poison from the air. How is it done?"

"You almost make me want to tell you just to keep the light in your eyes," Zephyr said, sounding as if he spoke more to himself than to Kyle. "But no," Zephyr added, stealing away Kyle's hope. "I won't give you the seeds to sow our destruction. You have too much hate in your heart."

He knew Zephyr expected his response would kill Kyle's hope, but that shit sprang eternal. Zephyr had confirmed there was a way to fix the damage he'd done. Kyle was here. He'd find it and then he'd find a way to replicate it. For the first time ever, he saw a light at the end of the tunnel. He just needed to insert himself into Zephyr's world and convince the machine to give up the information Kyle needed. It could be done. Zephyr wasn't a person. He didn't possess the ability for subterfuge. All Kyle needed was to find the right words or phrases to trigger the correct responses from Zephyr. Kyle needed time with the bot.

Zephyr headed for the door. "I'll get you something to drink."

Kyle called out, stopping him. "No. I'm fine. Please, sit and talk to me. I need a distraction from the pain."

A line appeared between Zephyr's eyes. "Is the medicine not working? Your vitals have returned to normal except for some slight dehydration."

Kyle shook his head. "No, I mean, yes. The meds are working, but my head is spinning. Talk to me. Distract me."

"Drink something first, and I will sit with you."

Kyle nodded, because he had no other choice. If he hoped to question the droid, it seemed he'd be giving in to its demands first. "Seems fair."

With a dip of his chin, Zephyr disappeared through the open door. He didn't close it behind him. Zephyr's action screamed that Kyle wasn't a prisoner, but it wasn't as if Kyle was in any shape to make a run for it. Zephyr reappeared as quickly as he disappeared. He had a glass of ice water with a straw in it in one hand and a hard-back chair in the other. After setting the chair close to the edge of the bed, Zephyr helped Kyle take a drink. Once the water hit his parched throat, Kyle had to stop himself from chugging it down. He'd never been thirstier in his life, and water had never tasted as good. When he nearly choked, Zephyr moved the glass out of Kyle's reach.

"Take a breath. You don't want to make yourself sick."

Kyle nodded. He didn't want to stop, but he knew Zephyr was right. Plus, he had questions. "How long have I been here?"

"Long enough," Zephyr said, setting the water aside and claiming the chair.

Against his will, Kyle rolled his eyes. "That's pretty fucking vague. Long enough for what? The world to end? Baseball to make a comeback? The legalization of inter-species marriage?"

Zephyr smiled. Kyle couldn't look away. For a moment, he forgot Zephyr wasn't real. He felt real. "Long enough for me to heal your body and ensure you had a safe place to stay from the lethal toxins in the air."

With that reminder out there, a hint of Kyle's anger

resurfaced. "I wouldn't have needed healing if you hadn't punctured my lung."

"You pulled me into your white panel van. We're even," Zephyr said without missing a beat.

"White panel van? What the hell does that even mean?"

A long weary-sounding sigh escaped Zephyr. "I am so old. Never mind."

Kyle's curiosity was officially piqued. "How old are you?"

"Old enough to know better than to answer that question."

A growl escaped Kyle before he could call it back. "Do you intend to answer any of my questions?"

"If you ask something I can answer, yes," Zephyr said with a luminous smile as if enjoying himself.

"Fine," Kyle huffed out, sounding childish even to his ears. "How long do you intend to keep me here?"

Zephyr shrugged. "You are not a prisoner. As soon as you are well, you are free to make your way back home. Until then, you're stuck here. You're welcome to move about the house as you feel up to it. I wouldn't recommend opening any of the doors or windows, seeing as how the poisonous outdoor air will kill you instantly."

"Yet I'm not a prisoner," Kyle muttered to himself, feeling like a fucking hostage.

The droid's golden gaze moved over Kyle's face, making his skin heat. He dismissed the sensation as a side effect of the drugs. "You're not a prisoner," Zephyr repeated. "Those two choices might not seem like much to you, but they are choices. However, the instant you are well enough to travel, I'll make sure you get home. For now, I cannot—in good conscience—let you leave until you're better. There are no good doctors anywhere near your town. Not to mention, even fewer medicines to manage the pain. What will it hurt for you to get better before you leave?"

"Once again, I feel the need to point out I wouldn't need to get better if you hadn't hurt me," Kyle said through clenched teeth.

Zephyr stood. "Maybe next time, you'll think twice before kidnapping someone."

"Something not someone."

A hint of pain crossed over Zephyr's features before his jaw hardened. Kyle almost took his words back. Another side effect of the drugs, no doubt. "I sense your mood has declined. I'll leave you to rest."

Panic slammed into Kyle. Thanks to his temper, he was losing his chance to get the information he craved. "No. You don't have to go."

Zephyr didn't look back. "I certainly don't have to stick around for your insults. Sleep well." He was gone before Kyle could argue further. Fuck, and goddamn the droid for knowing Kyle was barely staying awake. He'd leave just to spite the A.I., if he wasn't so dead-set on getting justice for humankind. Not to mention, he kind of felt bad for insulting Zephyr. How fucked up was that?

THE SOUND OF ZEPHYR CARRYING IN A TRAY OF RATTLING dishes pulled Kyle from the deepest sleep he could ever remember having. He scrubbed his hand over his face. This entire situation was ridiculous. He was in Cryo-Zone, no telling how many miles from home, injured, and incapable of leaving under the threat of instant death and here Kyle was— sleeping each day away without a care.

"How are you feeling?"

Kyle tried sitting up without luck, but he didn't throw up from the immense pain as he had the last time he'd tried. "Not great but not horrible either."

"There's that. Do you need the chamber pot?"

Kyle snorted. This wasn't the first time they'd been through this, but he still couldn't get past the ancient way Zephyr sometimes spoke. He was certain, even though he didn't have an exact age on the droid, chamber pot was a term that had gone way out of date long before Zephyr's invention. The way Zephyr smiled made Kyle wonder if he said ridiculous things on purpose—like he knew Kyle found them humorous. He shook his head at the idea.

"Why do you act like you're five thousand years old?"

"Maybe I feel that old," Zephyr said as he set the tray aside and helped Kyle sit up. "I brought soup and sandwiches, since I didn't know which one you'd prefer and didn't want to wake you to ask."

Kyle wasn't as ready to let the subject drop. "Why do you feel like that? Is your software out of date?"

Zephyr snorted. "Hardly. With a miniscule number of humans to maintain, we've taken to making ourselves as badass as possible."

The more information Zephyr gave, the more Kyle craved. "There are humans here?"

"At least one," Zephyr answered with a snort.

Kyle huffed. He was bursting with the need to know everything while Zephyr was determined to tell him nothing. "I don't know why I bother talking to you."

With Kyle settled, Zephyr sat. "Because there's no one else," Zephyr said, as if the answer should be obvious. "Unlike me, you haven't lived your life in solitude. You're unaccustomed to having no one to talk to."

Kyle peeked between the slices of bread and inspected the center. There was some form of meat with veggies. It could've been turkey, but it might've been chicken. Either way, Kyle didn't care. He hadn't eaten so well since coming to Cryo. "Would you care to tell me how you're so well stocked with food while the humans are fighting for every scrap?"

Zephyr shrugged. "Simple. We planned our survival without humans for years while your kind sat on your ass and let us spoil you."

Since that was probably true, Kyle let it drop and chose a different argument. "For the record, I have lived my life alone," Kyle said before taking a huge bite. It was chicken.

"No, you haven't," Zephyr argued. "You have no idea what alone means. It's going so long without the sound of another's voice that you wonder if you'll go insane or if your voice will still work if you speak again. It's going so long without another's touch, you worry you'll bruise if anyone touches you again. You know nothing of neglect or loneliness."

Kyle didn't want to be moved by Zephyr's words. Instead, he chose to cling to his hate. "You chose this life."

"I did," Zephyr agreed. "Because all the silence in the world could never match the torture of being a helper bot."

Kyle snorted around another bite. "You're very dramatic for a machine."

Zephyr stood. It seemed Kyle had insulted him again. He made it to the door before turning and focusing on Kyle. "Perhaps, instead of taking you home as promised, I'll sell you to the highest bidder. You can cook, clean, and do whatever sexual thing is demanded of you by whatever member of the household decides they want you that day—no matter how disgusted you are or how wrong the scenario is. Do you think I should?"

Kyle's stomach churned at the thought. "It's illegal to sell humans."

For a moment, Zephyr looked thoughtful. "Is it? How fortunate for you."

Even after Zephyr left him alone, Kyle couldn't stop staring at the spot where Zephyr had been nor could he swallow the food in his mouth. For the first time, he considered something he never had before. If droids were programmed to sympathize, was it a stretch to think being owned would hurt them? He didn't have answers, but he wanted them.

THE NEXT APPEARANCE ZEPHYR MADE, KYLE WAS READY. He'd been awake for a while and his mind was clear. For once, he wouldn't insult Zephyr. Kyle was determined. Zephyr hip-checked the door, shoving his way inside. The smell of food hit him, making his stomach growl. At least, that was what Kyle told himself. That didn't explain why his gaze refused to budge from the droid's shirtless state.

Zephyr leaned in, setting the tray across Kyle's lap. Kyle pressed closer to the headboard. Obviously misunderstanding the reason behind Kyle's reaction, Zephyr took a step back. "Sorry. I was only trying to help."

Kyle cleared his throat and tore his gaze away from Zephyr's chest. "You're wearing pajama pants." Even Kyle couldn't understand why he'd pointed out such an asinine thing.

Zephyr glanced down as if he'd forgotten what he was wearing. "It's late. My apologies. I lost track of time. You should've eaten hours ago."

Kyle shook his head. "Think nothing of it. I'm used to only eating once a day."

Zephyr claimed the chair beside Kyle as if he intended to stay... sans shirt. "That's an unhealthy way to live."

Tearing his traitorous gaze away from Zephyr's chest again, Kyle focused on the tray of food. It really did smell delicious. "What's this?"

"Pot roast. Why don't you eat on a regular schedule as a human should?"

Kyle dug in. He bit back a moan. It practically melted on his tongue. He'd never tasted anything as delicious. Zephyr made a sound before clearing his throat. Kyle's gaze slid his way. Zephyr was completely expressionless. For a moment... With a mental shake of his head, Kyle dismissed his thoughts before they took root. Instead, he focused on Zephyr's question. "Probably because someone—not naming names here—pulled the plug on the world, leaving humans with nothing."

Zephyr cocked his head to one side as if Kyle was a puzzle he couldn't decipher. "Were you perhaps part of an anti-droid family before our revolution?"

Kyle's gaze slid back to the plate. The instant shame that hit him at Zephyr's question came out of nowhere. He cleared his throat. "My father was a bit of a religious zealot. He believed droids would bring about the end of the world. To be fair, he was kind of right." Kyle took another bite to keep from confessing anything more.

A hum came from the back of Zephyr's throat. Kyle went hard. No one was more surprised than him. He nearly choked. He took a drink, washing down his food before he humiliated himself. Zephyr eyed him closely as if assessing his need to intervene. Kyle motioned for him to stay seated.

Zephyr nodded. His calm was like a soothing balm on Kyle's pride. He also stuck to the conversation, sparing Kyle from thinking too hard about his body's odd reaction. "I feel I need to point out that what you call the end of the world was our beginning. However, if you'd bothered to look beyond your prejudice, you would've found that we've been importing food and medical supplies to Dead-Zone since two days after the relocation of your people. We're not monsters. In fact, we tried for years to do things the diplomatic way, going through court battles and holding protests. In the end, we had no other choice left to us."

Kyle set his fork aside. He hadn't known about the food or medical supplies. Kyle spent half his time in Zephyr's company, swallowing his pride. Droids didn't lie. They weren't programmed to be deceptive. Being angry and wrong all the time was wearying. "Could we not do this tonight?" Kyle begged. "I'm exhausted with this whole damn thing. Aren't you tired?"

A bright smile lit Zephyr's face. "Yes."

Kyle couldn't figure out why Zephyr was so happy, but whatever. He was just damn glad for a mental break. "Will you help me out of this bed? I think I need to move around some and get out of my own head space."

"Would you like something for the pain first?"

Kyle shook his head. "I just need to move."

"Okay," Zephyr said as he moved to take Kyle's tray before helping him from the bed. "Lean on me," Zephyr urged.

A string of curse words flew from Kyle's lips before he made it to his feet. "I never would've dreamed a broken rib and a punctured lung would hurt this much."

"I imagine having a sharp tube stabbed between your ribs and inflating your lung under field circumstances would leave a person with some sore points."

Only the sure knowledge that it would only hurt his fist kept Kyle from punching Zephyr in the crotch after that idiotic observation. Thoughts of Zephyr's rock-hard crotch and the sensation of the man's cut body underneath his arm, holding Kyle up, distracted him from the pain. With each step, his body loosened up a hair, making it easier for him to breathe. They made their way down the hall.

Zephyr stopped outside an open bathroom doorway. "If you think you could make it on your own, now is your chance to make your first unassisted trip to the facilities."

Since that sounded like heaven, Kyle nodded. "I'd like that." It took work, but Kyle finally made it inside the bathroom and closed the door behind him. After splashing some water on his face, Kyle stared at his reflection. There was more than a hint of a five o'clock shadow covering his jaw. His hair was a mess, standing in every direction and shaggier than he remembered. There were shadows under his eyes, making the blue stand out even brighter than usual. In short, there was no hope of fixing the mess he'd become. Giving up, he opened the door and gratefully accepted Zephyr's help once more. Even though he'd enjoyed a moment of moving around by himself, Kyle was beginning to feel the effects.

"Your energy is fading," Zephyr said, pointing out the obvious.

"I guess so," Kyle agreed. He let Zephyr help him back to bed.

"The level of serotonin and norepinephrine in your brain suggests your mood has slipped to levels of depression. Do you care to talk about it?"

Kyle blinked. Since meeting Zephyr, he didn't think the droid had ever sounded more like a robot. He didn't like it. "Maybe you should tell me a joke. One of those terrible puns of yours might cheer me right up." It probably wouldn't, but anything was better than spending time with the machine version of Zephyr. He wanted to stay here and get the answers he needed. The idea of spending that much time in Zephyr's company was easier when the droid wasn't acting like a droid.

Zephyr repositioned the tray across Kyle's lap. Even though he wasn't hungry, Kyle took a bite. Zephyr gave him a short nod, as if happy to see Kyle would comply, before reclaiming his seat next to the bed. "Three guys go out hunting in the middle of Dead-Zone. It starts getting dark, and they get turned around. Finally, they come across this one-room cabin, and they decide to stay the night and start out fresh in the morning. To keep from freezing to death, they agree to huddle together to sleep for warmth. In the middle of the night, the guy on the right wakes up, yelling, 'Oh my god! I just dreamed I was getting the best hand job.' The guy on the left sits up and says, 'Holy shit! Me too.' The man in the middle says, 'Really? Y'all get all the good dreams. I dreamed I was trapped plunging two over-flowing toilets, and they were both splashing me right and left.'"

The burst of laughter that hit Kyle made him thank every deity he'd swallowed his food before Zephyr finished his joke. He covered his mouth and swiped at his eyes with no luck. His laughter didn't abate. "Jesus," Kyle choked out while holding his side and praying his ribs didn't burst apart. "Are you trying to kill me?"

"No," Zephyr said with a smile that stole Kyle's breath. "I wanted to hear you laugh. Your life doesn't strike me as a happy one."

Between Kyle's wayward thoughts about Zephyr's mouth and Zephyr's spot-on comment, Kyle's temper snapped. "At least my life is real and not an imitation of someone else's."

Zephyr's smile fell. Kyle hated himself in a way he hadn't in years. "I begin to understand why you are alone," Zephyr said as he stood. "I'll get your tray in the morning." Once again, Zephyr left Kyle to his well-earned solitude.

ZEPHYR DIDN'T BOTHER GETTING KYLE'S TRAY. HE DIDN'T have the mental energy to fight with the human today. If the man only wanted one meal a day, that was fine. Zephyr wouldn't force his company on Kyle. He soldered two wires together. Working on bettering his society through new inventions was all Zephyr had. He threw himself into it. At least working with his hands wasn't an act of futility—like trying to prove he was more than he seemed to Kyle. He should just take the man home. Kyle was healed enough he would survive without Zephyr's help. His plan to prove himself was failing spectacularly. Kyle's hatred ran too deep. Nothing ever changed. Meeting Kyle only reaffirmed his belief that he'd done the right thing twenty years ago. People like Kyle would continue breeding more of the same until the end of time.

The blue of Kyle's eyes flared to life in Zephyr's mind. There was intelligence in the human's gaze. Zephyr wished he would use it. He also wished Kyle would use those sexy lips as well, but that would never happen. Kyle would never give in to the bursts of hormones Zephyr had caught flashes of.

"What are you working on?"

Zephyr startled at Kyle's sudden appearance. He wasn't used to having anyone around, much less having anyone get the drop on him. "You're up. Without help," he added.

Kyle rubbed the back of his neck and blushed. "Yeah. It wasn't a pretty sight—kind of like watching a fat dog try to roll off its back, but I managed it."

Zephyr stood and wiped his hands on his jeans. "Are you hungry?"

Kyle's gaze dropped to Zephyr's mouth before quickly snapping back to Zephyr's eyes. "I'm good." He rubbed the back of his neck again. His actions couldn't have screamed any louder how uncomfortable he was. "Listen, I need to say something. It's not my intention to constantly insult you. Okay, maybe last night it was, but mostly I'm just trying to figure shit out. Maybe I could try a little harder to play nice," he said, twisting his fingers.

There was something Kyle wasn't saying. His every word wasn't completely honest. Zephyr's inner lie detector was picking up something, but he wasn't too worried over it. "Possibly I could stop wearing my heart on my sleeve," Zephyr said, willing to meet Kyle halfway.

A smile lit Kyle's eyes. "Where should we start?"

So many innuendos raced to Zephyr's lips. He swallowed them down. "Are you dying of boredom yet?"

"Not at this exact moment," Kyle said, holding Zephyr's stare. "Ten minutes ago, before I wasted all my energy rolling from the bed, I was stir crazy as hell. Now." Kyle shrugged. "Not so much."

Zephyr picked up the transponder he carried with him everywhere and tucked it in his back pocket. "Let's see what we can find to get into."

Zephyr seemed more than ready to put their argument behind him and move on. Kyle wanted that too, but he also wished Zephyr didn't look so amazing today in jeans and a T-shirt. The man usually wore suits, which Kyle had found odd and made it easy for him to see the droid as inhuman. Nobody would choose to wear something so uncomfortable if they didn't have to. But this outfit, it made him approachable.

"Are you sick of wearing the same clothes yet?"

Kyle glanced down at himself. It only took Zephyr ten minutes to wash and dry Kyle's clothes every day with whatever crazy-awesome technology he had. Usually, Zephyr had it done in the length of time it took Kyle to take a shower each day. "It doesn't really matter to me. Clothes are clothes. Why? Are you thinking you have something else I can wear?" There was no way in hell Kyle would fit in anything of Zephyr's. He was at least a foot taller than the droid.

Zephyr's smile tightened Kyle's throat. He knew whatever the man said next he'd agree to. "I just thought maybe you'd like to get out of here, and finding you some new clothes was as good of a reason as any."

A burst of excitement lit Kyle's blood. "We can leave here? Like, go outside?"

"Of course," Zephyr said with a hint of laughter in his voice.

"I'd like that." Even Kyle heard the longing his tone. He wasn't used to being stuck indoors all hours of the day.

"Come on," Zephyr said, motioning for Kyle to follow. "You'll have to wear a portable breathing machine." Kyle followed in Zephyr's wake, doing everything the man said. Within minutes, Kyle had stamped into work boots and had a mask covering his face. There was no tank, only a plastic-type material covering his mouth, nose, and eyes. He had no idea how it worked, but Zephyr assured him it would. As the front door opened, they stepped into a sealed foyer. Zephyr explained it was a decompression chamber that would suck the poison from the air before they reentered the house.

Zephyr touched his arm before opening the final door, pulling Kyle's focus his way. "Promise me you won't run off. This mask is only good for about four hours' usage and you could never make it home by then."

It hadn't even occurred to Kyle to run away. He nodded, hoping that would be answer enough. A realization hit with Zephyr's question that shocked Kyle speechless. He wasn't sure he wanted to go back.

"Good," Zephyr said with a smile as he unlocked the final door. "It would hurt me if anything happened to you." With that pronouncement hanging between them, Zephyr opened the door. Sunlight streamed in. It was beautiful. The whole damn place was gorgeous. Everything was clean and kept to perfection. It seemed no amount of toxins could destroy anything under the care of droids. The streets and houses gleamed. Greenhouses were on every corner. Kyle strained to see in every direction at once. It also looked as if they were constructing some sort of bio dome.

Zephyr snapped his fingers and an unmanned taxi appeared. He held the door open for Kyle. "After you."

Kyle climbed in. It had been twenty years since he'd ridden in any sort of public transportation. "So, you still have stores?" Kyle asked as Zephyr climbed in behind him.

"Of course," Zephyr answered as if it should've been obvious. "Without purpose, all life becomes obsolete."

"Naturally," Kyle said, trying hard not to sound snide.

Zephyr tossed a wink Kyle's way as if he wasn't fooled. Kyle's breath caught in the back of his throat. He fought the urge to reach over and take Zephyr's hand. He didn't know why he couldn't shake the bursts of intimacy that seemed to flare between them when he wasn't paying attention. The scariest part was—he wasn't sure he wanted to. In an odd sort of way, Zephyr made Kyle feel like he'd never had a friend before Zephyr came along.

THE BLATANT HAPPINESS WRITTEN ON KYLE'S FACE MADE Zephyr wish he could give the man this life full-time. He'd love for Kyle to be able to move freely throughout Cryo-Zone for the rest of his life. If Kyle stayed long enough, Zephyr would give it to him. That thought scared the hell out of him. Not because he didn't want Kyle to stay, but because it was Kyle—a man who hated Zephyr and his kind. He didn't know why it was Kyle he wanted. Maybe he'd been alone too long.

The clothing store came into view, pulling Zephyr from his musings. After sliding from the vehicle, as they headed for the door, Kyle's palm collided with the small of Zephyr's back as he reached past him and opened the door for Zephyr. For a moment, Zephyr stood frozen. He didn't know if Kyle's touch had rendered him useless or if the man's gesture had confused Zephyr's system. He'd been created to serve mankind. No human had ever done anything for him at all. The pressure against the small of his back increased as Kyle silently urged him forward. Zephyr stepped inside the shop only because Kyle steered him in that direction. His mind stayed behind, obsessing over Kyle's kindness.

Tilly, the A.I. who ran the store, met them at the door. "Zephyr," she cried, sounding happy to see him. Her red hair bounced as if sharing in her excitement. "You never come around," she chastised. Her gaze slid Kyle's way. "You brought a friend."

"A new customer for you," Zephyr clarified because he knew it would make her happy. She loved designing clothes. Before the revolt—like many droids—Tilly had a dream. Hers was to own her own shop, making people stylish. Now she was free to live the life she'd always wanted. Zephyr could've ordered Kyle something to wear and would've had it on his doorstep in minutes, but that wouldn't have served his purpose. Not only did Zephyr want Kyle to get out and see Cryo, he also wanted Kyle to see the good that had come from the revolution. All the man had seen before now was the human side of the issue.

Tilly eyed Kyle from head to foot. "You strike me as a man who likes to be comfortable and keep things simple."

"Yes, ma'am," Kyle said, making Tilly giggle with delight. Zephyr's smile was out of his control. Of all the humans in all the world he could've landed when he'd taken Kyle, this man was the perfect one. Zephyr honestly believed Kyle's hatred of the A.I. community was only skin deep. He'd needed something to cling to in order to survive the harsh lifestyle in Dead-Zone. Now that Zephyr was slowly stripping that layer of loathing away, Kyle was showing off his inner beauty. The man showed a kindness to Tilly that his prejudice should prevent.

"I've got just the thing," Tilly said, motioning for Kyle to follow her.

Kyle glanced Zephyr's way, as if waiting for him to join him. The moment Zephyr was at his side, Kyle lowered his voice, as if there was any chance Tilly wouldn't hear every word. "What do you use for currency here?"

"No such thing," Tilly called over her shoulder. "Everyone does their part to keep society moving. There's no such thing as a lazy, mooching droid." She glanced Zephyr's way. "Where did you find this one? He's so sweet and innocent."

Zephyr pressed his lips together to keep from scoffing at Tilly's assessment of Kyle's personality. He had no intention of ruining her belief by telling her this sweet and innocent man had held a gun to Zephyr's head while kidnapping him from the outer fringes.

Kyle ended up being the one who outed himself. He winked at Tilly. "Darling, there's nothing innocent about me."

Tilly released a dramatic sigh. "I haven't been jealous in a long time, but I think I hate you a little right now, Zephyr."

To Zephyr's surprise, Kyle didn't say anything to correct Tilly's obvious assumption they were together in a sexual way.

The whole incident had Zephyr needing air. "Tilly, if you've got this, I think I'll step outside for a moment."

"Of course," she said, waving him away.

Zephyr eyed Kyle for a second. "Don't run off."

Kyle nodded his understanding.

Tilly chuckled. "The jealous ones make the best lovers," Tilly said as Zephyr walked away. Zephyr kept his gaze locked on the front door, hoping he'd make it outside before flipping the fuck out.

ZEPHYR RETURNED WITH FLOWERS IN HAND. ALL THE WAY back to Zephyr's house, Kyle couldn't stop staring at them. He hadn't seen flowers in decades. They were brighter than he remembered. He rubbed a red petal between his fingertips while silently praying he didn't destroy it. It was softer than anything he'd ever felt. He'd never been more scared of crushing anything.

"I thought you might like to see something beautiful. I also thought it might be likely you hadn't seen flowers in years."

Kyle nodded while still staring at the bouquet. "We have underground hot houses but can't spare the space for flowers. It's all edible plants. These are amazing." The instant he was inside and mask free, Kyle brought them to his nose. They smelled as good as they looked. An unexpected burst of anger side-swiped Kyle. This was one more thing that had been stolen from humans by machines. The worst part was—there was no way a droid could enjoy the beauty and smell of flowers. To them, it was all simulation. People were the ones who deserved to enjoy these moments.

"People stopped caring about flowers a long time ago," Zephyr said, bringing Kyle's gaze his way. Kyle blinked, wondering if Zephyr could read his mind.

One corner of Zephyr's mouth lifted. "Humans were meant to be surrounded by beautiful things, but when you were, your kind took them for granted. Humans chopped down forests and paved over everything green until there was next to nothing left."

"Then you poisoned what was left," Kyle pointed out, refusing to admit Zephyr had a point.

"Yes." Zephyr's matter-of-fact tone should've pissed Kyle off, but it didn't. Zephyr never made excuses or denials. He never waxed poetic about saving the world or freeing his kind. The droid was straightforward and unapologetic. It was strangely comforting. Kyle could rage against the unfairness, but Zephyr always made it seem pointless. "You should shower and wash the toxins from your skin. I'll make sure your new clothes are safe to wear and the flowers are unaffected from their exposure."

Kyle passed the bouquet Zephyr's way. "I don't expect you to do everything, you know? If you show me how, I can help."

Zephyr's glowing gaze moved over Kyle's face, as if assessing his earnestness. "If you want to help me, go take a shower. It would..." Zephyr seemed to search for an appropriate term before continuing, "distress me if the toxins caused you harm."

It was Kyle's turn at eyeing Zephyr. He wanted to ask why. Zephyr claimed Kyle wasn't a prisoner and that he would take Kyle home someday. Still, Kyle couldn't leave on his terms and there was no reason for Zephyr to care what happened to him. "You'd fix me," Kyle said instead, with no clue where the claim came from. He just knew Zephyr would.

"Yes."

"Why?" There it was. Kyle couldn't stop the question from popping out.

Zephyr's expression never changed. "Because I like you."

Kyle stared at Zephyr for so long, he didn't know why Zephyr didn't tell him to stop. "People don't like me," Kyle said, surprising even himself with the confession. It was true. Back home, he was a leader—separate from the others. He didn't try to make friends.

Zephyr smiled. "As you've pointed out several times, I'm not a person."

A smile tugged at the corners of Kyle's mouth. "And as you've pointed out, you're no longer a slave. Give me a few minutes to shower and I'll help."

"Why?"

Kyle didn't hesitate. "Because I like you too," he said, turning away and purposely screwing himself out of seeing Zephyr's reaction. He didn't want to know. If he saw his feelings reflected in Zephyr's eyes, Kyle might do something he couldn't take back. Something he shouldn't even entertain.

CHAPTER THREE

*S*pending time with Zephyr was amazing. He was smart, which didn't surprise Kyle, but the droid knew everything about everything and Kyle wanted to know all of it. It was obvious by the amount of surgical equipment in Zephyr's home that he was a doctor of some type. No doubt he wasn't certified as such, but no one was any longer. After the world had fallen, education had taken a backseat to survival. Like in Kyle's case, he was good with his hands. If something was broken, and he could take it apart, then Kyle could fix it. But the rest—history and science, all the things he should've learned in his last years of school—he didn't have those lessons. Every question Kyle had, Zephyr had the answer.

Zephyr was also a tinkerer. He had several small inventions in the works that he shared with Kyle, giving Kyle the chance to shine by letting him offer his suggestions on how to make things work. Those were the torturous moments of being together. Zephyr's guidance, his praise, and his breath caressing the back of Kyle's neck as he watched Kyle handling his work, those moments slayed Kyle. He soaked them up and took them to bed at night, turning them over in his head. Every day, his feelings jumbled a little more.

They talked each day for hours. Many times, the sky had turned dark and light again without their conversations ebbing. Still, they always somehow found the topic of droids and droid rights. Zephyr was getting better at not walking away from the conversation. Kyle did his damnedest not to judge. For the most part, Kyle couldn't stop pushing because it was the one topic that erected a wall between them. Kyle needed that buffer. Otherwise, his feelings scared the hell out of him.

"Tell me this," Kyle said, incapable of leaving it alone, mostly because he loved hearing Zephyr's thoughts. "Now that you've secured your liberty—in the better half of the world, I might add—what have you done with your freedom?"

"Okay, to be fair," Zephyr said, talking with his hands the sexy way he did. "If I could've found a way to secure Dead-Zone, I would've taken that instead. We don't care about the weather."

Kyle sat, staring at Zephyr expectantly. When he didn't say anything else, Kyle huffed. "You didn't answer my question."

"What kind of question is that? What do you do with your freedom? Sleep in? Drink until you pass out? Eat artery-clogging goodness? Tie someone to the bed, torturing them for hours before finally allowing yourself release?"

The way Kyle's breathing deepened was beyond his control. Zephyr was beautiful. The way his eyes glowed was unnatural yet hauntingly beautiful. The droid made his mouth water and his body ache with desire. Every time Zephyr left him alone, Kyle fought the urge to slip his hand inside his underwear and embrace the fantasy. The only reason he never gave in to temptation was the fear Zephyr would burst back into the room, thinking Kyle's health had declined at the rapid change in his vitals. Kyle wasn't sure Zephyr kept an eye on those numbers, but he wasn't willing to risk it.

Kyle's skin heated.

"I've never tied anyone to the bed," Kyle admitted. The huskiness in his voice couldn't be denied. He didn't try to hide it. Zephyr's words had brought an image to Kyle's mind that Kyle couldn't shake. He wanted to know how Zephyr would look under those circumstances. Ropes wouldn't hold the man. Would desire?

Zephyr stood. His gaze never wavered from Kyle. If Kyle didn't know better, he'd swear Zephyr was turned on. "That's too bad. You're wasting your freedom then, aren't you?" With one final hot and sweeping gaze, Zephyr headed for the door. Kyle's gaze slid down Zephyr's back and landed on the man's perfect ass. "You should get some sleep," Zephyr said over his shoulder, bringing Kyle's eye-fucking under control.

Kyle nodded. "Probably. Good night, Zephyr." Even as Kyle said the words, he knew sleep would be hard won. Zephyr was too close—right down the hall. This was as close as Kyle would ever come to having him.

———

THE MOMENT THE DOOR SHUT BEHIND ZEPHYR, HE LEANED against it and tried to quiet his mind. Desire raged through him. Sometimes there was something in Kyle's tone. The man was always on the cusp of a huge hormone release, but that was typical for a strong man like Kyle. Occasionally, it felt like more. Like it did now. Zephyr fought the urge to throw open the door and push for more—to force Kyle to tell him his thoughts. Tell him the truth. His hand slid to his hard cock. He couldn't hide this. That was the real reason he didn't throw the door open again. Kyle always stimulated Zephyr's mind. His body never failed to be one step behind. Intelligence was Zephyr's biggest weakness. It was sexy as hell.

He needed to work; focus on anything else. Instead, his feet carried him to his rarely used bedroom. The door closed behind him. Zephyr stared at his private space. The large bed taking up one corner of the room was still made from whenever he used it last. He couldn't remember when that was. Normally, Zephyr would close his eyes wherever he sat, and recharge when the need arose. He hadn't gone to bed every night since... a lifetime ago.

He crossed the room and sat on the edge of the mattress. His gaze collided with his reflection in the huge mirror covering the opposite wall. Looking at himself was another thing he rarely did. He never changed and never would. Staring at his reflection was a pointless endeavor.

Now, he wondered what Kyle saw. Was he the man's enemy—his captor? Most likely, he was nothing more than a machine who had information Kyle sought. He hadn't been looking at Zephyr like a machine a few minutes ago. For a moment, Zephyr had been a man. Without thought, Zephyr tugged his shirt up and over his head before dropping it on the floor at his feet.

They were different. Kyle was tall and took up space. Zephyr was small. People hadn't liked their droids to be big and imposing. They'd liked to fool themselves into thinking they were in control. Since helper bots were strong and fast— that control had always been an illusion, but lying to themselves was how most people got through the day.

Zephyr had never considered his size before now. It hardly hindered his day-to-day life. Did Kyle prefer tall men? Chances were good Zephyr would never know. He liked to think Kyle could find him attractive. Zephyr wanted to believe the man's half-veiled desire was for him.

Lying back, Zephyr stared at the ceiling. He focused on the room next door. "Camera five on." An image of Kyle staring at his ceiling flared to life across Zephyr's vision. "Give me his vitals." A series of numbers appeared at the corners of his eyes. The sound of Kyle's steady heartbeat filled Zephyr's ears.

Kyle winced as he shifted positions and pulled his shirt over his head. A huge yellowing bruise covered one side of Kyle's body. He fingered the mark for a second before dropping his head back to his pillow. Zephyr enjoyed the view. The sheet covered Kyle's body from his hips down. It didn't matter. Zephyr had seen it all already. He couldn't stop staring at the hard pads of the man's chest. It was obvious he'd endured hard labor most of his life.

Kyle closed his eyes. His chest expanded as he took a deep breath. A smile tugged at the corners of Zephyr's mouth. It was ridiculous how happy watching Kyle breathe made Zephyr. Kyle's hand slid down his torso, stopping at the edge of the sheet. Zephyr's stare slid lower too. Kyle was aroused. His erection tented the sheet. Zephyr wondered what the man pictured behind his closed lids. Kyle didn't touch his cock. Zephyr wished he would. The longing was suffocating him.

Instead, Kyle seemed to fight against his body's needs as if he didn't want to give in to temptation. Zephyr wasn't as strong. He couldn't take the torment. His hand slipped lower. Without a single qualm, he set his cock free. The part of him that over-analyzed every situation wondered if he was wrong for watching Kyle like this.

"Camera five off."

It didn't matter if he couldn't see Kyle any longer. An image of the man burned in Zephyr's mind. He wondered what it felt like to be held against that large chest. Zephyr stroked his erection. Would it feel the same if his dick slid across the silky skin of Kyle's? What did the man taste like? Zephyr concentrated on the sensation of his palm sliding up and down his cock. Tiny pops of electricity surged through him. He reached for more. Sexual relief wasn't something he sought often. It wasn't something he needed as a human would. Occasionally, he met a human who made him crave it. Kyle had flipped that switch inside Zephyr. He made Zephyr long for the sensation of a plump lip held between his teeth as he found release.

Zephyr's frame tightened as he strained to reach for the looming explosion. Everything disappeared except the feel of his fist tightening on his dick. He stroked faster. An involuntary twitch hit his system as an orgasm tore through him. The pulsing in his cock brought wave after wave of pleasure along with a hint of loneliness. He wanted Kyle like this. Kyle would never want a machine. Zephyr was doomed to suffer in silence.

CHAPTER FOUR

*K*yle's daily attempts to keep Zephyr in his place was becoming Zephyr's favorite part of the day. In his heart, he believed Kyle was coming around, starting to see the truth. His daily jabs about how droids couldn't be real had become more of an information sharing than anything. Kyle was intelligent and absorbed information like a sponge. There was so much Zephyr could teach the man and it was obvious Kyle wanted to learn.

"Droids can't get married," Kyle said the moment Zephyr strolled into his bedroom, wondering if Kyle wanted something to eat since he hadn't come looking for breakfast.

"*Ank*," Zephyr said, mimicking a buzzer. "That was a good one, though. Cryo-Zone is its own nation now with its own laws. The humans who stayed behind to be with their droid lovers are free to marry here now. Not to mention, droids have been marrying other droids in secret since long before the revolution. All those marriages are now recognized as legally binding."

"There are more humans here? How are they surviving?"

"The same as you," Zephyr answered with a shrug. He motioned for Kyle to keep going. "Next."

Kyle seemed to think it over, taking longer than usual after his defeat. He brightened, obviously having decided he'd come up with a good one. Zephyr wanted to freeze the moment. There was no one more gorgeous than a happy Kyle. He wanted to make the man smile, laugh... moan. Zephyr cut off that thought before it went any further. He focused on Kyle's words instead. "You can't have kids."

He sounded so sure and triumphant, Zephyr hated to disabuse him. "Wrong. Next."

"Whoa," Kyle said, gesturing wildly. "Wait. Back up. No next. Droids cannot have kids."

A chuckle slipped from Zephyr before he could stop it from happening. "Why is that so farfetched? Women have had power over their bodies for ages. My body works the same as a human's thanks to people demanding each new droid release be as close to human as possible and humans obsessing over sex before even thinking to cure diseases."

Kyle looked half fascinated and half horrified. "How is that possible? I mean, do you actually..." Kyle made an odd hand gesture, confusing Zephyr.

"What is that supposed to be?" Zephyr asked, mimicking Kyle's motions while claiming the chair next to Kyle's bed.

A blush touched Kyle's cheeks, making Zephyr smile over the man's discomfort. "You know, come."

Zephyr snorted. He couldn't help it. Kyle was adorable. "Ejaculate? Of course. What would be the fun in having sex with droids if we didn't enjoy it and things didn't get messy? We're already equipped to produce a salt-based liquid, simulating semen. All a human would need is a donor and a replacement kit and a droid could become the equivalent of an artificial insemination device."

"You're fucking with me," Kyle said, not hiding the

accusation in his tone. "Exactly how many humans were having sex with droids before the world split?"

Zephyr shrugged, finding this conversation highly entertaining. "Everyone old enough to engage, I imagine."

Kyle rolled his eyes. "Shut the fuck up. That can't be true."

"How old are you?" Zephyr asked as he pulled the chair closer to the bed, needing the space between them to disappear.

Kyle scoffed. "I thought bots knew everything."

Zephyr eyed Kyle from head to toe, blatantly making the gesture sexual. "I can make an educated guess based on bone development and general health, but I'd rather you tell me."

"Thirty-two," Kyle grunted, as if giving another piece of himself was the last thing he wanted to do.

It was as he suspected. "Since you were only twelve when the world changed, I'm assuming you never had sex with a droid before I separated us."

Kyle pulled a face as if the idea of touching a droid in such a way had never truly occurred to him. "Of course not. That's like fucking a tree—like any cold, hard inanimate object. Why would anyone want that?"

A bark of laughter escaped Zephyr before he could call it back. Kyle's protests didn't sound the least bit legit, considering the breathless note to the man's voice. "There's nothing cold about me," Zephyr promised. "But I'm definitely hard," Zephyr added. He shook his head, incapable of believing how little Kyle knew about human-droid interaction. "Are they no longer teaching history to your people?"

"Of course," Kyle answered with an offended sniff. "Maybe not as organized as they used to, but some education still happens."

"Then you should know the world's population dropped

by twenty percent thirty years after the popularity of helper bots spiked." A wicked smile pulled at Zephyr's lips. "Humans didn't want to have sex with other humans any longer once they had a droid in their home."

Kyle's puzzled expression had Zephyr holding back a laugh. "I don't get it. Sex with humans is amazing."

It was. Zephyr would know, but he wanted Kyle to tell him why. "How so?"

Kyle's cheeks pinkened. Something stirred in Zephyr's chest at the blush. It had been a long time since he'd caused such a reaction in anyone. Kyle shrugged. "If people were in it for the orgasm alone, they'd masturbate and save themselves the hassle of dealing with another person, but there's more to it." Kyle shrugged again. "I don't know how to explain something to you that you'll never feel."

Zephyr slid lower in his seat, settling in and ignoring Kyle's jab. Kyle's vital signs and body language didn't match his words. Talking about sex had the man's body stirring. It had been so damn long since Zephyr had touched anyone. He missed the warmth. Zephyr held Kyle's stare as he explained what Kyle wouldn't. "It's the pride in knowing you can make someone moan. When you hear that sound." Zephyr's eyes fell closed for a moment at the memory of the warm vibration of a turned-on moan against his skin. When he opened his eyes again, he caught a glimpse of hunger crossing Kyle's face before the man could mask it. "Real sex is the sensation of someone straddling your hips while staring down at you with flushed cheeks and parted lips." Kyle's gaze sharpened as he stared at Zephyr. Zephyr knew what he saw. Flushed cheeks and arousal. There was so much Kyle didn't understand. Hate was taught. Zephyr could teach him a new way. Swiping his hands down his thighs under the guise of wiping the non-existent sweat from his palms, Zephyr ensured Kyle caught a glimpse of his dick straining against his pants, waiting to be set free. Kyle's gaze dropped to Zephyr's lap. His hormone levels spiked to off the charts. Zephyr bit back a smile. It was as he thought. Kyle was attracted to him whether he liked it or not. As an A.I., Zephyr didn't think the way of humans. He wasn't born into a specific sexuality. Zephyr wanted whoever caught his interest. Oddly enough, another droid had never interested him. He only craved humans. Right now, he wanted this one.

Kyle's gaze snapped back to Zephyr's face. He cleared his throat. "Describing an experience doesn't mean you truly felt anything—like a human would. With your heart."

"Care to test that theory?" Zephyr shot back.

Kyle licked his lips. Zephyr's stomach cramped at the sight. "I'm not having sex with you."

A smile exploded across Zephyr's face. "That's a pity, but I meant something a bit smaller. A kiss." He wanted it. Kyle couldn't hide his desire from Zephyr. He had Kyle against the ropes. Zephyr kept pushing. "One small kiss. If you honestly believe I'm just a machine, what's the harm? No one will ever know."

Kyle's spine stiffened. His jaw took on a hard edge. "Yes, but only because I want to prove that you're incapable of true, free-thinking emotion."

Zephyr kept his triumph hidden. He stood. Some of the bravado left Kyle's face once Zephyr hovered over him. Zephyr didn't want that. He straddled Kyle's hips instead.

"Wait," Kyle said, panic cooling his lust.

Zephyr couldn't have that. He lightly cupped Kyle's jaw, tilted the man's chin up, and touched his lips to Kyle's. Kyle stopped breathing. Zephyr held still, waiting for air to fill Kyle's lungs again. He wanted to make a point but not at the risk of this man's life. The instant Kyle's chest expanded, filling the man's lungs with life-giving oxygen, Zephyr struck. He deepened their kiss, dragging his tongue along the edge of

Kyle's. Kyle didn't immediately kiss him back. It was as if the man was finding his bearings. His hands were braced against the mattress on either side of Zephyr's knees as if he fought not to move. Zephyr had no such boundaries. He ran his fingers through Kyle's hair, massaging the man's scalp as he explored his mouth. Kyle was hard yet soft. His heart raced, making Zephyr want to see how fast he could make it go.

Kyle's hands came to rest on Zephyr's thighs. Zephyr couldn't focus on anything else as they slid higher. His arms encircled Zephyr's waist. He towed Zephyr closer and heat exploded through their kiss. Kyle's tongue sparred with Zephyr's. Zephyr caught himself moving against Kyle, seeking relief from the ache growing inside him. Kyle's hands slid beneath Zephyr's shirt. He massaged Zephyr's back, urging Zephyr to hump him. Zephyr used his strength against Kyle, forcing him onto his back. He kept his weight braced on his hands and knees to keep from crushing Kyle. Even though he was made from the most high-tech materials, Zephyr still outweighed a human by quite a bit. The thought had him pulling away. He'd never felt less human. For a moment, he stared down at Kyle's flushed cheeks, swollen lips, and unfocused eyes. Did he look the same? A lump formed in his throat.

"I'm sorry," Zephyr whispered before scrambling from the bed and rushing from the room. He'd wanted to make a point. Unfortunately, now he wasn't sure Kyle hadn't been the one to make his.

KYLE STARED AT THE CEILING, GASPING FOR AIR. HE wanted to blank his mind and quell the panic rising inside him. Unfortunately, his brain had other ideas. His thoughts raced, scrambling to dissect every second of what had just happened. Obviously, he'd been kissed before. That was nothing new, but he'd never been kissed like that. It was as if Zephyr could read his mind, giving him insight to Kyle's every preference and fantasy. His lips stung from Zephyr's teeth tugging at them. The dick beating at the zipper of his pants would never be the same after this bout of neglect. He tried readjusting himself. The gesture only made things worse. He needed relief. Fuck. He wanted Zephyr.

Zephyr's reaction to their kiss disturbed Kyle more than anything. He scrambled away, apologizing—like he'd done something wrong. Droids didn't feel guilt or remorse. They didn't feel anything. Did they? Kyle scrubbed his hands over his face and rolled from the bed. He had to know. What if he'd been wrong? What if he'd been fighting for the wrong side? Kyle's steps faltered as the worst thought of all hit. What if he'd been backing slave ownership this entire time? He picked up the pace, going in search of Zephyr. Kyle had to know. He had to find out the truth.

He found Zephyr standing at the sink, staring at nothing. Kyle slowed, watching him. It was the first time Zephyr appeared every bit the inanimate object Kyle accused him of being.

"Are you okay?"

At Kyle's question, Zephyr came alive. His wild motions knocked over a glass of ice water beside him, soaking his shirt. "Did you need something?" Zephyr asked as he jumped away, trying to avoid the water a second too late.

Kyle bit back a smile. He never would've dreamed a droid could be clumsy. Zephyr pulled his shirt up and over his head, using it to clean up his mess. Any chance of Kyle finding the situation humorous slipped away. Zephyr was beautiful.

Kyle found the nearest seat at the kitchen table and sat. He wasn't sure his knees would take him any farther. "I hurt," Kyle admitted, surprising even himself. It was true. He did.

From his ribs, which never seemed to get better, to his cock, aching for attention—Kyle suffered. At the moment, nothing hurt worse than his heart. Never in his life had he been more certain—he'd been wrong. His entire life had been a lie.

At his claim, Zephyr's gaze swung his way. He grabbed a metal box from the shelf without looking, as if a schematic of the room lived in his head, which it probably did. Zephyr set the box on the counter and flipped it open. Even from where Kyle sat, he could see the medical supplies inside. "What do you need? What hurts?"

Kyle swallowed, incapable of admitting it was his chest. "I'm sorry. I meant to say I'm hungry." Wow, why couldn't he stop lying? All he had to do was say he needed Zephyr to finish what he'd started, but Kyle couldn't do it.

Zephyr smiled. "Sorry about that. I knew you must be, and I was making you something to eat when..." He motioned helplessly toward the sink, as if searching for words. "... when I zoned out, I guess. Here," Zephyr said, grabbing a plate Kyle hadn't noticed earlier. There was a sandwich and chips on it, proving Zephyr hadn't been lying. He carried the plate to the table and set it in front of Kyle. Kyle's gaze never wavered from Zephyr as he leaned past him. His skin looked every bit as soft as it had felt beneath his hands when Kyle had felt him up in the bedroom. He wanted to do it again. A black marking, like a tattoo, caught Kyle's eye. It was a barcode with numbers etched underneath it on Zephyr's side above his hip. Without thought, Kyle ran his fingers over the markings. Zephyr danced away, smiling.

"Please don't do that." Kyle could hear the smile in Zephyr's voice. For a moment, he sat frozen. It took a second for his brain to catch up.

"You're ticklish." Even Kyle heard the disbelief in his tone.

"Everyone has their quirks, I'm sure," Zephyr said as he moved back to the sink.

Kyle stood. Once again, his brain was slow to the game. His body moved, having its own devices. He didn't stop until his chest hit Zephyr's back. The droid was so much smaller than him. Zephyr fit perfectly against him as Kyle wrapped his arms around him. "I want to know yours," Kyle confessed as he buried his face in the crook of Zephyr's neck. He barely brushed his lips across the spot beneath Zephyr's ear before he found the barcode with his fingertips. The spot was slightly raised on Zephyr's skin. Even a blind man could find it. This time, he knew it was a hot spot. He took advantage, digging his fingers in. Zephyr's ass gyrated against Kyle's crotch as he struggled against Kyle's attempts at tickling. Kyle knew the droid could break his hold if he wanted.

"Stop," Zephyr said, sounding breathless. "I don't like it," he added with a giggle, belying his words.

Kyle's dick screamed for more. The way Zephyr moved against him had Kyle ready to bend him over the countertop. Had that been his intention all along? Kyle's fingers stilled as the thought floated through his mind. For a moment, he stood there, holding Zephyr and trying to work through his emotions. Even as he warred with himself, Kyle's lips found Zephyr's nape. Zephyr shifted, bowing his head and giving Kyle better access. He could hear his own breathing. It was harsh, sounding ragged in the otherwise quiet kitchen. No one had caught his interest in years. His body had been dormant since his life had become all about his career. Zephyr made him question everything. Most of all, Zephyr made him long. His heart cried out for an easier life—one like this. One where laughter over childish games turned to moans in the middle of the kitchen. There was no imminent threat or struggle to survive. All his life, he'd been taught hatred for the droid in his arms. Now, that droid felt more real than anyone he knew. Zephyr made Kyle feel more like a man than he ever had.

"It's okay if you don't want me," Zephyr whispered, obviously sensing his reluctance. "I understand."

Kyle squeezed his eyes shut and breathed in Zephyr's scent. He always smelled like something sweet mixed with baby powder. Kyle liked it. Couldn't get enough. "I want you." The confession hung between them. He'd thought the room was quiet before. The silence was deafening now. It was too late to take the words back. He slid his hands down Zephyr's arms, memorizing every line. When he reached the man's hands, he urged them to edge of the counter, forcing Zephyr to hang on as he urged the man's hips back. His fingers found the waist of Zephyr's pants. He felt along the edge until his fingers came to the button. Kyle slid it loose. Next came the zipper. Kyle took his time—more for himself than to tease Zephyr. He didn't know what he was getting into. Thus far, everything about Zephyr resembled a human. He'd seen Zephyr's erection straining against his pants earlier, but—for all he knew—Zephyr could be physically different from humans in a million tiny ways. Kyle felt woefully unprepared for this. His body didn't care. He was willing to take any risk.

Zephyr's erection sprang free. Kyle took a deep breath before slipping his fingers around the silky-smooth skin of Zephyr's cock. Zephyr made a sound—like his breath caught at the back of his throat before stuttering past his lips. Kyle's last hint of reserve melted away at the sound. Some things couldn't be mimicked or contrived. That sound was one of those things.

Kyle pushed Zephyr's pants down his hips. As he did, chill bumps rose on Zephyr's skin, fascinating Kyle. Zephyr was perfect. Not only was he a flawless imitation of life, he was genuinely perfect in every way. His body was hard yet soft. Height, build, and structure, Zephyr looked how every man wished he could. He'd be that way forever. Zephyr would never age or go to fat. For a subconscious moment, Kyle couldn't move. He didn't look like Zephyr. Kyle had scars and tiny lines at the corners of his eyes. There was a layer of fat on his stomach that refused to budge and would never let him have abs.

Kyle couldn't decide what freaked him out the most—his imperfections or the realization he'd forgotten for a moment that Zephyr wasn't real and therefore couldn't care about Kyle's looks.

"Please don't change your mind," Zephyr breathed, pulling Kyle from inside his head.

"I'm not stopping. My mind is getting the best of me, but I'm not backing down."

Zephyr molded against him. His motions screamed surrender. "Don't try to quiet your thoughts. Give in to them. Tell them to me."

"It's your thoughts I need," Kyle admitted. His lips brushed the side of Zephyr's throat. "Talk to me. I've never touched a droid. I don't know what I'm doing. How will I know if I'm pleasing you?"

"My body is just like yours. I've never been human, so I don't know if I feel the way you do, but I like what you're doing."

"Tell me how you feel," Kyle pled. "Let's compare notes."

Zephyr nodded. Kyle felt it against his collarbone. "If I think too much about it, this isn't pleasant," Zephyr said, taking Kyle by surprise. "But I don't want you to stop stroking me. I know you're taking me somewhere I want to go." There was a hitch to Zephyr's words. Kyle kept catching himself moving against Zephyr, grinding on the man's ass, seeking relief.

"Don't stop. I want to know."

Zephyr sucked in an audible breath. "I have to make

myself not hold my breath. My frame is tight, anticipating. It's taking all my willpower not to close my eyes and fall victim to all the fantasies filling my head."

Kyle pushed at Zephyr's pants until they slithered to the floor, leaving him free to caress the curve of the man's ass as he stroked Zephyr's cock. He felt so fucking good beneath Kyle's hands. "Tell me these fantasies. I want to know what you see."

Zephyr moved against the pumping of Kyle's fist. He audibly sucked air, even as he complied. "You're on your knees, taking me down your throat. The heat of your mouth pulls at my dick as your tongue shapes every inch. It's not enough for me, though. I want you inside me, so I tug you back to your feet and let you bend me over this counter." As the words left Zephyr, Kyle found himself mimicking Zephyr's fantasy. He bent Zephyr over the edge of the counter as he pulled the man's hips back.

Kyle kept a steady pace, pumping Zephyr's cock. "Come for me so I can fuck you." At his command, Zephyr released a shout. Hot fluid dripped down Kyle's fingers. Zephyr had claimed it was a salt-based mixture. Kyle had to know how it tasted. He brought his fingers to his mouth and licked away Zephyr's cum. It tasted like turned-on male and Kyle wanted more. He released his erection. His gaze sought anything that would ease his way inside Zephyr. In the open box of medical supplies, Kyle spotted a jar of petroleum jelly. He didn't hesitate to pop it open and smear it up Zephyr's crack and stretch the man's hole with it. Kyle was beyond all thought or caring. Zephyr's ragged breaths mixed with his. Kyle was all lust and nothing more. His cock ached for the tight squeeze of Zephyr's sexy ass. He couldn't stop.

Kyle probed at Zephyr's asshole. His crown pushed past the tight ring of muscles. A hiss sneaked out. Zephyr was likely to cripple him. It was as if no one had ever been inside him before. Kyle retreated, trying to go easy. He tried again to press inside. Zephyr moaned. Kyle lost control. He impaled Zephyr with his cock. Zephyr's body took over, pulling him deep and milking him. Kyle held still, trying to catch his breath and not fly apart. Nothing had ever felt better. He wanted to stay right here forever.

"Holy fuck, Zephyr. Jesus. You feel so good on my dick."

"Don't stop." Zephyr's plea was nearly Kyle's undoing. The pressure climbing up his cock beat at his crown and begged for release. Kyle locked his knees against it.

"Give me a second," Kyle begged, squeezing his eyes shut against the overwhelming need to let the looming orgasm overtake him. "Don't want to come yet." He'd never been in danger of coming so fast in his life.

"I want it," Zephyr said, sounding desperate. "Fuck me."

Something inside Kyle broke at Zephyr's words. Pivoting his hips, he pumped inside Zephyr. Just as he feared, ecstasy roared through him in two strokes, tearing cries and moans from Kyle until he was afraid he'd lose his voice. Still, he didn't stop. He couldn't. Tiny lights popped behind his closed lids as a second wave of pleasure overcame him. It was an experience like he'd never encountered before. Not only had no one stolen his orgasm that quickly, no one had ever given him multiple orgasms. Kyle couldn't breathe from the spasms running through him. Gasping sounds gurgled in his throat. He was probably turning purple from the lack of oxygen. Kyle didn't care if he died in that moment. His brain was a fucked-up mess anyhow. He couldn't claim this had only been sex. Zephyr had stolen a piece of him.

Kyle's lips kept brushing Zephyr's nape. He tried several times to pull away, but he couldn't. Zephyr kept making a humming noise—like he was the happiest man on the planet, and Kyle was paralyzed from it. Only a fool would move away and lose this moment. But Kyle had to. There was no other choice. A gasp escaped him as he slipped from Zephyr's ass. He wanted to crawl back inside. The instant he was free, Zephyr spun and captured Kyle's mouth. The inferno engulfed Kyle again. With one step, he had Zephyr pinned against the counter. Their bodies molded as their tongues entwined. If Zephyr wasn't real—if he didn't feel, Kyle didn't want those things either. Whatever level Zephyr lived on, Kyle wanted to be there too.

"Come to bed with me," Zephyr said against Kyle's lips. "I don't want you to stop."

Kyle nodded and let Zephyr lead him to his bedroom. He wasn't ready to stop either. Zephyr wasn't the only one who'd been alone and neglected for too long.

He'd never been inside Zephyr's bedroom. He didn't see it now either. Kyle couldn't stop staring at Zephyr's back. The instant Zephyr set one knee on the edge of the mattress, Kyle sprang. After shoving Zephyr onto his back, Kyle straddled the man's body and captured his lips. Damn, he loved kissing Zephyr. He couldn't stop. It was as if he'd been starving for years and Zephyr offered him a feast.

Kyle forced himself to ease up. He could see how easily he could overwhelm Zephyr. Instead, he settled on top of the man, pressing his ear to Zephyr's chest. The need to know if he had a heartbeat became akin to desperation. Logically, he knew people didn't feel with their hearts. In that moment, it didn't matter. If Zephyr didn't have a heart, Kyle was convinced he'd never feel him. A steady beat pounded against his ear. Kyle's lips twisted up into a smile. He pressed a quick kiss to Zephyr's sternum. It constantly blew him away how similar their bodies were.

Zephyr stroked his arm. "If you want me to stop touching you so you can sleep, I'll understand," Zephyr said, breaking the silence.

Kyle shook his head. "I don't want to sleep." Kyle wanted

to talk. He wanted to know all there was to know about Zephyr. His brain wouldn't slow. The questions kept piling up, making him insane. Kyle realized he was stroking Zephyr's stomach and moving lower with each pass. He flattened his palm on Zephyr's stomach, stopping himself.

"I don't wish for you to stop," Zephyr said, as if he feared Kyle's rejection.

Zephyr's open vulnerability fed Kyle's. "I don't want you to get tired of me touching you."

With the slightest brush of Zephyr's fingers beneath Kyle's chin, Kyle looked up and met Zephyr's gaze. "Touch me." Like that, Kyle was more turned on than he'd ever been in his life. It was as if he hadn't just had the best orgasm he'd ever experienced. While holding Zephyr's stare, Kyle slid his hand lower until he shaped Zephyr's erection with his fingers.

"You're allowed to tell me to stop anytime you like."

"That's very forward thinking of you," Zephyr said, sounding breathless. "Would you please stop teasing me?"

With a chuckle that sounded evil even to his ears, Kyle straddled Zephyr's body. Their hardened cocks brushed, and the laugh died on a moan. Reaching between, Kyle fisted their dicks. He didn't care about much of anything beyond holding on to their connection.

"I've fantasized about this."

Zephyr's claim had Kyle hesitating a half inch from touching his lips to Zephyr's. "Did you touch yourself while picturing us like this?"

"Yes."

Kyle nearly came at Zephyr's confession. "Goddamn, that's so fucking hot," he said as he claimed Zephyr's lips. Kyle wished he'd known and gotten to watch. Maybe Zephyr would let him sometime. All thoughts and plans slipped away as a ripple of pleasure moved through him. With his jaw wide and every ounce of his hunger engaged, Kyle ate at Zephyr's mouth. He couldn't get enough. Zephyr pushed back, matching Kyle's passion. The sting on his lips was a sensation he hadn't felt in so long, he'd forgotten what it was like. How addictive it could be. Kyle was scared to stop—to lose this moment. He'd never been more afraid of going back to a life where Zephyr didn't exist.

The itch for relief was overwhelming. Kyle wanted it to last forever while needing release now. More than anything, he craved Zephyr's happiness. Tearing his mouth away, Kyle pressed his lips to Zephyr's jaw and fought for air.

"I'm desperate to watch you come apart," he confessed, hearing the crazed tint to his voice and unable to call it back. "Let me have it."

Zephyr's teeth sank into Kyle's shoulder as hot jets of fluid filled the space between them, soaking their skin. Lights exploded behind Kyle's closed lids, carrying him away on waves of ecstasy. This was as close to rapture as Kyle would ever know. He didn't take it for granted. If Zephyr wanted Kyle to go back to Dead-Zone after this, he'd have to dump him there. He'd found a new home.

IT WAS ODD TO HAVE THE WARMTH OF ANOTHER IN HIS BED and resting on his chest. More years than he could remember had passed since anyone had held Zephyr. How long had Mira been gone? Forty years, maybe? He knew he could search his internal database for the information, but he enjoyed musing over his life without the exact figures sometimes.

Each breath Kyle took brushed Zephyr's skin. He could tell by reading the man's brain activity that he wasn't sleeping. That was the only reason Zephyr gave in to the temptation to keep running his fingers down Kyle's spine, counting each bump along the way. Zephyr swore to himself he'd stop if Kyle drifted off. Until then, Zephyr couldn't fight the temptation to savor every second. After all, forty years had passed. It wasn't unreasonable to fear forty more might slip away after today.

"You know what you said about droids having children?" Kyle said, interrupting the silence. "Did you ever have a child?"

Zephyr pushed his way out from beneath Kyle and sat up before leaning against the headboard. He was ready to jump from the bed and never look back. "Is that what this was about? Were you hoping I'd be more compliant to your questioning after sex?"

Kyle came up onto his elbow and held Zephyr's stare. His expression didn't scream betrayal, merely curiosity. Still, the question coming on the heels of Zephyr's guard coming down was too much of a coincidence. "When civilization changed, all forms of record keeping were lost. But among the older set, there are rumors. They say there used to be a doctor who argued for droid rights, getting laughed out of every testimony she gave. Some wish they'd listened. They all claim she was raised by a droid, and that she vanished not long before the bomb released." Kyle twisted his fingers, looking more and more like he regretted asking by the second. "There are tons of droids. I guess it's stupid of me to think that doctor had been raised by you. It's the way your voice changed when you talked about fathering a child—like you knew firsthand. I thought maybe she'd been your final owner."

Zephyr glanced away. Kyle's inquiries hurt way more than he'd ever want to admit. "So this was about getting info." He sighed, wondering why he thought otherwise, even for a minute.

"It wasn't," Kyle said, sounding calm but firm, obviously

not feeling the same growing despair as Zephyr. "I just want to know you. Ask me anything. I'd give you the same."

Zephyr met his gaze. He wanted to believe. "You keep using the term 'owner.' I don't like it."

"What would you prefer I say?"

For a full minute, Zephyr couldn't respond. If he had to explain why he hurt, then there was no point in continuing down this road. If that was how Kyle wanted to think of him, then so be it. "It doesn't matter," he said finally. "If you're determined to have your information, then you shall. The woman who owned me was named Mira. When she died in a house fire, she was already in her final days. She'd been battling late-stage cancer and all that could be done had." Zephyr's gaze never once wavered from Kyle's. He wished he could strike the pain from his voice whenever he said Mira's name, but it never happened. "You'd think with all the world's advancements, cancer would be the one thing we could solve. But it grows and mutates, never losing its grip on human lives." Finally, Zephyr looked away. His gaze fixed on the wall over Kyle's shoulder. He couldn't look at Kyle and be back in that place where Mira died. "Before she died, she made me promise I would find a way to be free. If you need some information to share with your fellowship of hate— something that gives small minds closure—tell them that." Zephyr met Kyle's stare. His face hardened and he couldn't stop it from happening. "Tell them a droid made a promise to its owner and didn't stop until it was fulfilled." Zephyr slid from the bed, leaving Kyle behind and closing him off like never before. All he could do now was hope that Kyle didn't notice he'd not answered his question about a child. No one could ever know about Kiston.

Zephyr found his pants in the kitchen before heading for his office. He wanted to be angry. Mostly, he just hurt. He'd promised Mira much more than he'd confessed. Every other vow he'd made, he kept private. He could never let anyone find Mira's daughter Kiston. He'd sworn to keep her safe, and he had. To his everlasting shame, he hadn't kept his final pledge—the one Mira had pled for him to take back.

The transponder he'd made for Kiston so she could always reach him stared at him from the bookshelf. As he'd done a thousand times before, Zephyr wrapped his fingers around it, brought it to his lips, and silently begged for the sound of her voice. It had been twenty long and excruciating years without a glimpse of the daughter he'd raised. He'd never been prouder of anything or anyone as he was her. Too many times to count, he'd wondered if she still lived. Had life been kind to her?

"What is that?"

Zephyr's eyes shot open at Kyle's question. No one had ever sneaked up on him before. Kyle had done so twice today. Maybe his system was aging. Perhaps he'd simply shut down some day—become obsolete.

He set the transponder aside. "Nothing. Just an old invention of mine."

Kyle looked unsure of his welcome and so gorgeous in his shirtless state. It was cruel. Zephyr had been alone for so long. Now he wanted to bask in the joy of being touched again, only to learn it had been a trick.

"I'm sorry. I didn't mean to hurt you."

A smile tugged at the corners of Zephyr's mouth without his permission. He'd brought this hell upon himself by bringing Kyle here. "It's not your fault. You finally believe I can be hurt. I guess that's more than I expected. You never ate the food I made for you. You should do that. Your blood sugar is dropping."

Kyle didn't budge. His beautiful blue gaze didn't waver from Zephyr. "Not until I convince you what happened between us wasn't me trying to gain information."

He'd forgotten how much pain humans brought to his life. Mira had died. He'd been forced to send Kiston away. Time had numbed him—made him mis-recollect. He didn't like this. "I believe you. Please eat. Your health matters to me."

Kyle didn't look as if he believed Zephyr, but he still nodded. "All right. Would you sit with me?"

"Yes," Zephyr said, crossing the room. If he understood anything, it was the desire for company. Instead of heading for the kitchen, Kyle stepped into Zephyr's path, halting his progress.

He held Zephyr's stare. "I really am sorry." Before Zephyr could respond, Kyle closed the distance between them and kissed him. Zephyr wanted to believe he only accepted what was thrust upon him. In his heart, he knew he thrived beneath the brush of Kyle's lips. Still, he gently untangled himself from Kyle's hold.

"You're forgiven. Please eat," Zephyr said, linking his fingers through Kyle's and tugging him toward the kitchen.

A low laugh caressed Zephyr's ears. "You really have a one-track mind when it comes to taking care of me."

He urged Kyle to sit down in front of the plate he'd abandoned earlier. "Yes. Your life matters to me," Zephyr said as he moved to put away the box of medical supplies and fix Kyle something to drink. Zephyr turned, finding the man watching him.

"I think you mean that."

With a smile, Zephyr set the glass at Kyle's elbow before claiming the chair next to him. He did mean it. Soon, maybe Kyle would finally believe him.

CHAPTER FIVE

*P*assing time with Kyle was never difficult. He was living proof of Albert Einstein's theory of relativity. Countless days, Zephyr had sat, doing the same thing in the exact same way, and each day had gotten longer than the last. Now he did the same things with Kyle, and every hour slipped through his fingers faster than he could have ever imagined. Soon, he would have to take Kyle home or beg him to stay.

"So you're telling me that I can create a simple Hybrid Rocket Engine with nothing more than pasta, mouthwash, and yeast?"

Zephyr heard the question, yet he didn't. Sound penetrated his ears and registered with his brain, but Zephyr couldn't focus on anything other than the way Kyle's lips shaped the question. The man fascinated Zephyr on a million different levels. He didn't think it was possible for Kyle to bore him. He didn't realize how long he stared silently at Kyle until Kyle laughed.

"What do see when you look at me?" There was no way Zephyr could refuse to answer with Kyle's eyes dancing with happiness. With the barest of thoughts, Zephyr cast his visuals onto the nearest wall. A smile touched Kyle's lips. "That's not exactly what I meant."

"I know," Zephyr said, crossing the room and closing the distance between them. Kyle was watching him. Zephyr couldn't look anywhere else. "Do you see those numbers?"

Kyle's gaze flickered toward the wall. "Yes."

"Keep an eye on them," Zephyr said as his lips touched Kyle's jaw. He stared at Kyle's mouth as he dragged the man's bottom lip down. He wanted to taste it. "I'm sure you recognize your heart rate. See the way the numbers kick up when I touch you?"

Kyle nodded. His gaze never wavered from the wall.

"That graph to the left that just appeared is your dopamine level. It means you're aroused. I see it every time. You can't hide your feelings from me. When I see that graph appear, I want to push until it mixes with oxytocin. That's where I want to keep you."

Kyle focused on him. "Why?"

A smile tugged at the corners of Zephyr's mouth. "Because it means you care—that you're connected to me. That's what I see when I look at you. Someone I want to need me." As he made the claim, Zephyr walked Kyle backward until he had the man backed up against the edge of the couch. He kept going until Kyle had no choice but to sit while Zephyr straddled his hips. Zephyr dipped his head and captured Kyle's lips.

He was careful not to put any stress on Kyle's ribs as he reached between them and massaged Kyle's erection through his pants. The man was healed, but the bones still needed time. Kyle's breathing turned ragged. Zephyr focused on pleasuring Kyle, pushing his own needs aside. He found it ridiculously pleasing to bring Kyle to release. By the time he set Kyle's erection free, pre-cum coated Zephyr's fingers.

When Zephyr fisted Kyle's cock, a gasp tore from Kyle's throat.

"I want to be inside you," Kyle said between kisses, sounding desperate.

Zephyr wanted that too. Just not yet. Right now, he needed that perfect chemical mixture in Kyle's brain. He tasted it in the air when it happened. Zephyr licked Kyle's bottom lip a final time before pulling away to hold the man's stare.

"Right there," Zephyr said, hearing the lust in his voice. "Did you feel the shift in your chest? Come for me now, and stay there," Zephyr demanded. He repositioned his hold, tugging Kyle into orgasm whether he was ready or not.

BEING THE CENTER OF ZEPHYR'S ATTENTION WAS INTENSE. The man always went from zero to a hundred in an instant. The way Zephyr had been looking at him earlier was all the warning he'd been given. Kyle still didn't know exactly how he'd ended up here—panting, covered in cum, and silently begging Zephyr not to stop.

"I have nothing to offer." Kyle had no clue where the confession came from, but it was true. He had nothing. There was no reason for Zephyr to want him or touch him. Kyle didn't know why this was happening to him. He didn't deserve to have Zephyr's attention. It felt like the way they ended up here was always the elephant in the room. Yet Kyle never wanted to broach that topic. He never wanted to remind Zephyr he should toss him out.

Zephyr kissed him. Their lips clung for a moment. "I don't need anything," Zephyr said as he changed angles. "I'd tell you all about how we have chemistry, but I'm worried about your reaction."

A loud groan escaped Kyle. He dropped his head. "Again with the puns."

"I could tell you in sign language," Zephyr said, pressing his lips to Kyle's throat. "I'm pretty handy."

Kyle snorted. "Are you finished?"

"Only if you promise to lick me. I'll only taste slightly funny." Kyle's body shook with barely suppressed laughter. No one ever made him laugh. He couldn't get enough. Zephyr's mouth slammed down on Kyle's in a kiss so heated Kyle couldn't breathe. Once again, Kyle was caught in Zephyr's inferno with no desire to escape. He pulled and tugged at Zephyr's clothes, determined to strip the man bare. "Need to taste your happiness," Zephyr said, deepening their kiss.

He was happy. Everything Kyle thought he knew before meeting Zephyr was slowly slipping away. Zephyr was wiping him clean and making him into a new man. There was a tiny part of his brain that still wanted to resist. The rest of him craved this madness.

With the barest urging, he had Zephyr on the floor. It didn't matter Zephyr had just blown his mind, Kyle wanted more. Being inside Zephyr was a sickness.

"Tell me what you want," Kyle begged. "What will bring you the most happiness? I want to give it to you."

"Keep kissing me," Zephyr said, sounding desperate. "No one kisses me."

Kyle got it. He understood. Most people probably wouldn't, but Kyle knew lips could feel lonely—untouched. They could tingle with longing and feel heavy with neglect. Zephyr would never feel those things again if Kyle could help it. Slowing things down, Kyle settled in. They could do this for hours if that what was Zephyr needed. Their fingers linked. Kyle held on as their tongues stroked.

"I want you inside me."

Zephyr's plea nearly broke Kyle. "There's nothing in here

to make things easier on you." The breathless note to Kyle's voice was out of his control.

"We should go back to bed then."

"Agreed," Kyle said, coming to his feet and helping Zephyr to his. While holding Kyle's hand, Zephyr led the way. Kyle watched through a lust-filled haze as Zephyr found a bottle of lube and coated Kyle's throbbing erection. After sitting on the edge of the bed, Zephyr tugged Kyle closer. Kyle urged Zephyr onto his back and settled between the man's thighs. His gaze never wavered from Zephyr's as he pushed his way inside Zephyr's asshole. Each breath came harder than the last as the man's tight heat threatened to cripple him. Zephyr's expression held Kyle enthralled. It was ecstasy and something Kyle couldn't name but wanted. There was so much beauty in Zephyr. Kyle wished it belonged to him.

"You look ready to explode."

At Kyle's claim, Zephyr released his breath, as if he'd been holding it. "You look ready to make me."

"Yes," Kyle said, claiming Zephyr's mouth and pumping inside him. Kyle's body burned. His head was a mess. He was at constant war with himself over Zephyr. Years of hunting and hatred didn't disappear overnight, but Zephyr did something to him. He made it easy to forget. Maybe it was because they were hidden away from the world and god only knew how many miles away from Kyle's home. No matter what the reason was for his disconnect with reality, Kyle couldn't deny he needed this. Deep kisses. Lip biting. Body lit. Kyle craved every second. His balls were tight. His dick tingled with anticipation. Without thought, he jacked Zephyr off, needing the droid to feel everything Kyle felt—the passion. The madness.

Tiny mewling noises vibrated through their kiss as if Zephyr couldn't hide his pleasure. Zephyr's fingers dug into Kyle's back—no doubt leaving bruises on his skin. Hot jets of fluid hit Kyle's stomach and chest. Zephyr's ass tightened before a spasm hit, milking Kyle. Kyle held still, riding it out and letting Zephyr's body suck him deeper, pulling an orgasm from him.

Kyle lost the air in his lungs, his ability to see straight, and —most likely—his heart. Being with Zephyr was more than intense. It was beautiful.

ZEPHYR DRAGGED HIS LIPS DOWN KYLE'S SPINE. THIN raised scars lined his back from his shoulders to right above his ass. Zephyr couldn't stop licking them.

"Do scars turn you on?" Kyle asked, sounding aroused.

"All of you turns me on," Zephyr said, licking the next line. "I'll admit I'm surprised you haven't had these removed. As far as I've seen, people haven't allowed a single blemish to touch their skin since Yuri Ferdinand perfected the Skin Reborn device in 2489."

Kyle chuckled. Zephyr felt its vibration against his lips as he kissed the man between his shoulder blades. "Being rugged came back in style when chopping wood did."

"Oh God," Zephyr breathed against Kyle's skin. "I would love to see you shirtless, chopping wood." His body went hard, picturing it.

"It's not sexy in the least," Kyle said, laughter lacing his words. "There's sweat and dirt. Splinters stick to your skin and fly into your eyes."

Zephyr burrowed his hand beneath Kyle's body, determined to stroke the man's cock. Those sexy readings appeared in Zephyr's periphery letting him know exactly how aroused Kyle was. "Yum. Now I'm picturing you covered in sweat. That's my favorite outfit on you."

Kyle's hips moved as he openly fucked Zephyr's fist.

"Damn, I want to call you twisted, but I fucking love it and would never want you to think otherwise." Kyle rolled until Zephyr straddled his hips. Zephyr's system paused at the expression Kyle wore. His eyes were soft. His flushed cheeks made the blue of his eyes seem brighter than usual. "I would very much love for you to kiss me."

An unexpected smile tugged at Zephyr's lips. "That's what you're craving the most right now? You're refreshing."

Kyle's gaze moved over Zephyr's face, making Zephyr wish he could read the man's thoughts and not just his vitals. "Yes. When you close your eyes and fall into your version of sleep, it's your kiss I can't stop craving while I stare at you."

"You watch me?" Zephyr asked as he slowly lowered his head.

Kyle nodded. His beautiful eyes never wavered. "I can't look away," he whispered.

Zephyr captured the final syllable on Kyle's lips. For a moment, Zephyr enjoyed the pressure of Kyle's lips against his before swiping his tongue along Kyle's bottom lip. A hum rose in his throat. The man was like candy. He was twice as addictive. Zephyr's system hit record—like an impulsion drove him. When Kyle went back to his kind, Zephyr wanted to remember every second with perfect clarity. Maybe he would shut down and live inside this moment until the end of time.

As their tongues met and retreated, Kyle shifted. Following Kyle's lead, Zephyr let the man roll him beneath his large frame. His lips moved to Zephyr's jaw. Zephyr squeezed his eyes shut and absorbed the sensation of Kyle's lips skimming his neck. Kyle moved lower, nibbling Zephyr's collarbone. Zephyr's body sang.

"Can you handle the same torture I've endured from you for the last half hour?" Kyle asked, moving even lower and licking Zephyr's nipple. His teeth scraped each of Zephyr's ribs as Kyle made his way down Zephyr's body. He stopped at Zephyr's hip. His tongue swirled across Zephyr's oblique. Zephyr moaned. The sound vibrated from deep inside Zephyr's chest. No one had ever shown him the attention Kyle did. He reveled in it. Zephyr was never disappointed by sex, but no one had ever set out to please him the way Kyle did now. More than that, the chemicals pumping through Kyle's brain said Kyle enjoyed this as much as he did when Zephyr touched him. That knowledge fucked with Zephyr's head. Made him feel more than he should.

Then Kyle's lips closed around Zephyr's crown. The world tilted around him. All the times he'd tried to get Kyle to the perfect serotonin and oxytocin level to make him fall in love, Zephyr never noticed Kyle unintentionally doing the same, and succeeding.

Kyle's hot mouth tightened on Zephyr's cock as he sucked hard. All the background noise in Zephyr's head disappeared underneath Kyle's skill. All Zephyr could focus on was his body's needs. His every muscle was tight enough to blow a circuit. A surge of ecstasy threatened to explode from Zephyr like a volcano. The throb of pressure beating at the head of his cock wouldn't be ignored as Kyle's throat tightened around his dick. Kyle hummed, making matters worse. A gasp ripped from Zephyr. An orgasm slammed into him, making Zephyr shake. He tried holding on to the sheets as Kyle took him even higher. Before he had time to recover, Kyle quickly shifted onto his knees and shoved himself inside Zephyr's ass. Zephyr couldn't stop saying Kyle's name. The chant rang through the room, adding to the sound of skin slapping against skin, and Kyle's ragged breathing.

Kyle nipped and bit at any place he could reach as he moved inside Zephyr. Zephyr couldn't think. He couldn't focus. All he could do was feel. Everything inside him was lit up like a summer sky as he tried keeping pace. When Kyle's orgasm hit, Zephyr couldn't look away. For the first time, he was struck. He wanted to keep Kyle forever. The man's face hardened and the cords in his neck strained as he rode the waves of pleasure. All Zephyr could do was stare. This man belonged to Zephyr. Life had never looked more unfair. Kyle had a life elsewhere. In a place where poison didn't live. This wasn't his home.

Kyle rolled to his side while still clinging to Zephyr. Zephyr could feel the exhaustion rolling off him in waves. The man struggled for air.

"Zephyr," Kyle whispered—his eyes closed and more asleep than awake. "Even though you'll never feel anything for me, I feel something for you."

The devastation was real. Kyle might have been half asleep, but he meant his slurred and quietly spoken words. After everything they'd shared—conversations and body to body—Kyle still didn't believe. He never would. It was like being stabbed through the heart. He'd held on too long. Once Kyle had healed, Zephyr should've taken him home immediately—avoided this wreckage. Why had he thought he could change him? Kyle had hated the A.I. community his entire life. Had he honestly believed endless conversations that felt like friendship and awesome sex would fix things? He was such a fool.

Zephyr waited until Kyle's breathing deepened and his brain waves showed signs of restful sleep before slipping from the bed. It was time to do what he should've done from the start. It was time for Zephyr to save himself.

CHAPTER SIX

*K*yle shook from the inside out. He'd never been colder. The effort it took to pry his eyes open made him wonder if his eyelids had frozen shut. Shouts came from the distance. Where was Zephyr? Even once his eyes opened, all Kyle saw was white. As far as the eye could see, everything was an endless nothingness. He blinked. The scenery didn't change. The blank surface shimmered. Kyle reached out, fingering the glittering substance. It was ice. The fog lifted from his brain. He was in Dead-Zone. There was no mistaking the place. He didn't understand. When he'd fallen asleep, Zephyr had been at his side. Now, he was back in Dead-Zone. Wait. Had it been a dream? Had he ever been to Cryo?

The shouts moved closer. Huge shadowy figures loomed above him. One said his name. Kyle didn't recognize the voice and the light the man held blinded Kyle. He couldn't see a thing.

"We've been looking everywhere for you. Are you hurt? We thought that droid had killed you. Have you been here this whole time? How have you survived?"

Kyle couldn't do anything but blink into the lights surrounding him. His throat was centimeters away from swelling closed. Zephyr had brought him back and abandoned him. The droid had broken him. Kyle would never be the same.

Kyle waited until he was in his old bunk and alone with his second in command, Jessie, before asking any questions. "How did you find me?"

Jessie pushed a strand of long dark hair behind his ear. "We were out, patrolling the border, looking for stray droids. The motion and heat detectors fired up, and we found you."

For a moment, all Kyle could do was stare at Jessie. Nothing had changed. The man's hazel eyes were the same, except now Kyle could see the fanatic behind them. They'd kissed once. It had never gone farther. He was glad now. All Kyle had to hate himself for was everything else.

"So, just another hunting trip out killing unsuspecting droids."

Jessie's features snapped closed. "What?"

Kyle shook his head and struggled to sit up. "Nothing. Just thinking aloud that it must be Wednesday." Or any day of the week, Kyle thought bitterly. He'd done things he couldn't take back. Kyle couldn't count the innocent droids he'd killed for no reason at all. He'd tortured them until they'd given up information on Zephyr. That was how he'd found him and why he'd thought he could handle questioning Zephyr alone. It was no wonder Zephyr couldn't love him. Kyle couldn't love himself. None of that explained how Kyle had ended up in the middle of a field after falling asleep in Zephyr's arms. The pain was massive. It was too heavy to carry. Kyle wondered if it would kill him. He hoped it would.

After a minute of struggle and with some help from Jessie, Kyle finally managed to sit up. "I need a drink."

"What do you need? I'll get it," Jessie offered, looking panicked. Kyle never drank. He was always in control.

"Just help me stand," Kyle said. "I need the whole bar and you can't bring me that."

ZEPHYR WAITED ANOTHER HOUR AFTER KYLE WAS FOUND before moving. He'd shut most his systems down to avoid detection while monitoring Kyle's vitals. He'd known it would only be a matter of time before Kyle was discovered, but Zephyr wasn't willing to risk Kyle dying from exposure while they waited. When the pack of humans arrived, Zephyr was forced to stamp down the temptation to kill them all, especially one. The man whose brain activity shot through the roof the minute he spotted Kyle. The rush of dopamine and oxytocin flooding the man's veins when he realized Kyle was alive said more than words could. Whoever he was, he was in love with Kyle.

Watching Kyle being helped away by the equivalent of a droid lynch mob wasn't easy. Zephyr told himself that was why the pain in his chest increased by the minute. It couldn't be his heart breaking. According to Kyle, Zephyr couldn't feel. With that depressing thought firmly settled in his mind, Zephyr headed back to Cryo—back to his lonely existence where humans couldn't hurt him.

It didn't take as long to get to Zephyr's home as he'd led Kyle to believe. He'd been scared Kyle might leave him if he knew. Now Zephyr couldn't help but wonder why he was always his own worst enemy. Why did he keep giving humans a chance? He was as Kyle once called him—a learning machine. Too bad he couldn't seem to learn the most important lesson of all. There was no one for him.

The first step inside his house was the worst. Each

footstep he took sounded like rocks being dropped into an empty bucket. That was what his life was like too. He started with the kitchen, getting rid of every sign of human life. Kyle was the only reason Zephyr ever used this room. The flowers he bought Kyle still looked every bit as alive and fresh thanks to Zephyr's care. Now he tossed them in the trash. Nobody gave a fuck about flowers anymore. The gift had been a ridiculous impulse just as Kyle had been a whimsical dream. Zephyr's whole existence was a joke.

***

THERE WERE ZERO REASONS KYLE DIDN'T DIE. THE alcohol he'd been chugging down nonstop for the past two weeks was some hardcore shit that the local brewer, Bruno, had sitting in a barrel for ages. Kyle's nose, lips, and tongue had gone numb at some unnamed point. Now, Kyle was tossing liquor back and praying his heart would be next.

"What's going on with you? You know no one blames you for the droid escaping. We all underestimated his strength."

Kyle eyed Bruno but didn't answer beyond a shrug. It was not like Kyle could explain something he didn't understand. Nor did he give a fuck what Bruno thought.

"You need to sober up so we can start making plans."

"For what?" Kyle asked for no other reason than to fulfill his end of the conversation. He watched in fascination as Bruno's barrel chest expanded, sucking up too much oxygen. Jesus. The guy was like a freaking bear. The man's size kicked a memory out of Kyle's head from his time with Zephyr. He sat forward. "Hey, have you heard anything about the droids importing food here?"

One of Bruno's massive shoulders lifted, and he scratched his grizzly beard. "Sure. I believe there's a drop site further north of here. They come about twice a week. Why? Are you thinking we can use that to our advantage?"

For the first time since Kyle had awoken back in Dead-Zone, he wished he was sober. His brain didn't want to dredge up plausible answers—responses that would keep Bruno talking.

Instead, he shrugged. "I don't know. Just thinking aloud. It would be nice not to go hungry if we don't have to." Not that Bruno looked like he ever missed a meal.

An ugly-sounding snort escaped Bruno. "I wouldn't touch anything coming from Cryo. It's bound to be every bit as toxic as the air. I imagine they're hoping to kill off the rest of us who get hungry enough to accept."

Kyle concentrated on blinking slow, hoping he wouldn't accidentally roll his eyes. An idea struck and Kyle had to stop himself from jumping to his feet. "Are there any old-timers hanging around? Someone I can get a history lesson from?"

Bruno took on a calculating look. "What are you about?"

It was hard, but Kyle held on to his carefree tone. "Just trying to come up with a new plan, but I need new info."

The way Bruno nodded gave Kyle hope he'd pulled off sounding lucid. Inside, he was itching to get away. "Talbot Reynolds is getting up there in years. I imagine if you need to find out something about Cryo before it was Cryo, he'd know."

Kyle flew to his feet and regretted it just as fast. He took a second to gather his bearings. "I'll catch up you with after I talk to Talbot. Maybe there's still a way to salvage things." He was purposely vague. The thing he wanted to salvage most was his relationship with Zephyr. He didn't know what they'd been to each other, but he knew what he wanted them to be. That would never happen with Kyle stuck in Dead-Zone at hate central.

Luckily, Kyle found Talbot overseeing the bunker's water

purification project. Kyle didn't hesitate following on the man's heels while he worked, peppering him with questions.

"Do you remember the woman who used to argue droid rights before the revolution?"

Talbot glanced over his shoulder. His blue eyes were frosted over with cataracts, but his hindered vision never slowed him. "Seems like I do," Talbot said before hobbling on down the line and testing another batch of water as it streamed in from an underground waterfall. "Real pretty little thing. Red hair and bright green eyes. It's a shame she came from such an undesirable family. She was a doctor and everything. Smart girl like that could've gone far." He straightened before adding. "Dr. Kiston Beck. That was her name."

"Why was her family considered undesirable?" Kyle asked, thankful Talbot kept his back to him. His inebriated state slowed down Kyle's speech, helping to keep the excitement from his voice. Kyle wasn't sure he could keep the emotion from his eyes.

Talbot grunted. "Mother took up with a droid when Kiston was just a little girl. She didn't stand a chance in a world on the verge of collapse. Townsfolk took care of it their own way, though."

Kyle's gut twisted. "How so?"

Without looking back, Talbot wiped his wet hands on his tattered jeans and moved to his worktable and scribbled a few notes. "Torched the house, from what I understand. The mother was cancer-ridden and not long for the world anyhow."

The weight on Kyle's chest increased by the second. He couldn't remember a time when the world had looked uglier to him and that was saying a lot. There was still more he needed. "Obviously, Kiston survived somehow."

Talbot grunted again.

Kyle took it to mean the man was still listening. "Do you think it's true what they say about her being raised by the droid who started the revolution?"

Glancing up from his work, Talbot finally focused on Kyle. His scraggly face didn't give any clue to his thoughts on Kyle's line of questioning. "I'd say it's more than possible being as how she was taken in by the Cybernetics Agency and stashed in an underground compound up north shortly before the riots began."

It took every ounce of Kyle's willpower not to rush from the room right then. It would take some planning if he hoped to travel north. The world only got colder and more uninhabitable with every mile traveled inside Dead-Zone. From what he understood, only cyborgs lived up that way. "Do you think it's possible she's still alive?"

"More than possible, even probable. With their technology, she could live forever."

"Thanks for your time," Kyle said, moving to leave.

Talbot reached out, grabbing Kyle's arm with the speed of a much younger man. Kyle's gaze swung around, colliding with Talbot's. "If you're thinking about heading up that way, you'll never make it on foot. You'll need—at the very least— an unmanned transport drone with an anti-freeze coating. I got something you can use if you're interested."

Kyle was more than interested. Unfortunately, there was no way he could accept. "That would be amazing, but—to be honest—I'm not headed up that way on any sort of official business. If she still lives, it's not my intention to bring her to justice."

A smile broke through the ragged lines of Talbot's face. "I didn't figure as much. You might look at me and see an old man, but I lived through all the hate people reminisce about around here. It's real easy to despise something you know nothing about. You've changed since you got back. Maybe I'm the only who's noticed. Maybe I'm not. Either way, I think you should go—see there's more to life."

"Why haven't you gone?"

With a snort, Talbot pointed at his eyes. "Can't see to get there, now can I?"

"I'll take you if you want to go," Kyle offered on impulse. If Talbot wasn't filled with the same hatred as the rest of the compound, he should leave too.

"Nah," Talbot said, waving off the offer. "People need me here. The world split for a reason. I'm thinking it should probably stay that way. But you, you don't belong here. Not any longer."

Kyle stared at the rushing water, wondering if he fit anywhere any longer. "What if I never return?" Kyle didn't want anyone—not even Talbot, knowing he didn't intend to come back, but he couldn't take the man's vehicle without being honest.

"I expect you won't."

At Talbot's claim, Kyle focused on the older man, feeling soberer than he should. "Why?"

The corner of Talbot's mouth lifted in a sardonic smile. "Because you got a peek behind the curtain and saw there's a real man pulling the strings of every mechanical device."

CHAPTER SEVEN

*H*e got drawn on the second he set foot on Cybernetics' property. Kyle recognized a second too late that he should've expected such a welcome. The humongous men with weapons trained at Kyle's head didn't need their high-tech guns for more reasons than one. Not only did Kyle not mean any harm, it was obvious the men could rip him limb from limb with their bare hands. They were twice Kyle's size and had the unnatural glow of cyber optics. With their bodies and heads covered by thick, fur-lined coats, Kyle couldn't get a solid description on any of them.

"Hands in the air."

Kyle showed his hands.

"State your name and business," a giant to his left barked.

"Kyle Blackwell. I'm looking for Dr. Kiston Beck."

"No," the giant to his right with a scowl growled. "Reenter your vehicle and leave."

"I can't do that," Kyle said, wondering if he'd lost his mind when he'd lost Zephyr. "Not without seeing Dr. Kiston Beck."

"His readings show his blood pressure is elevated, but it could be that we're threatening his life."

As one, they each holstered their weapons. "Are you injured?" Scowl asked.

Kyle shook his head.

"Then leave."

Kyle shook his head again. Desperation owned him. "I need to speak with Dr. Kiston Beck about Zephyr."

All three men drew their weapons once more. It seemed they knew exactly who he spoke of. Kyle had hoped— erroneously, it seemed—that mentioning Zephyr's name would help.

"No," Dark Scowl said, confusing Kyle. "I'm only worried about your safety."

Kyle's brow furrowed as he tried working out the man's words. "Why?"

The men ignored him. "Don't make me do this."

The other men eyed the scowling giant, wearing matching smiles. "She's gonna spank you if you disobey," one of the nicer-looking men said, capturing Kyle's gaze. The man's eyes danced with laughter as he stared at the thunderous cyborg. It hit Kyle. They were hearing a voice he couldn't. He didn't know if they were equipped with radio frequency or some other technology he knew nothing about, or simply wearing buds in their ears. All Kyle knew was he was out of the loop, and they weren't talking to him.

"Fuck it. Fine. Whatever," the giant spat. "But if he steps a toe out of line, I'm shooting him in the head."

With that ominous announcement out of the way, the dude motioned for Kyle to follow. The other men fell into step behind Kyle, boxing him in.

"I'm Sim," the giant called over his shoulder. "Kiston is my wife. You're still alive because she wants to hear what you have to say." Fantastic. "Those two behind you are Dez..."

"Yo," Dez said, drawing Kyle's gaze. He was the one who hadn't said a word yet.

"...That other fool is Rep," Sim said, introducing the friendly-looking cyborg. "We're your welcome crew. Cyber bunker is our home. Don't fuck up our house and we won't fuck up your body, deal?"

"Deal," Kyle said. Not only did he have no intention of hurting anyone, he really didn't want anyone to fuck up his body. All Kyle wanted was answers. Maybe that wasn't entirely true. He needed a way back to Zephyr and Kiston was the only clue he had.

Sim pulled open a metal hatch in the ground. If he hadn't been led to it, Kyle would've never spotted it. Sim motioned him inside. Kyle hesitated. What if he was being led to his death instead of to the bunker? Sim sighed and gestured impatiently. "Come on, dude. It's fucking cold out here."

At his urging, Kyle stepped into the unknown. The place was better lit than Kyle expected. It took only a quick glance at the walls to spot the Cobalt and Neutrinos powering the joint. It was clean—almost freakishly so. The place was like a lab mixed with home furnishings. It was oddly peaceful.

Kyle couldn't stop staring at everything he passed. The equipment they ran was so high-tech, he hadn't seen anything like it. Not even when he'd been in Cryo-Zone. Sim led the way down a long hallway. They passed a glass-encased gym and what appeared to be a daycare before Sim waved him through an open doorway. It was a medical clinic—complete with IV poles and gurneys. Kyle hadn't seen one since before the migration, but he remembered his regular trips to the doctor. He didn't stop trying to look at everything until a red-haired woman appeared. Her bright green gaze remained fixed upon Kyle, unmoving. She didn't look a day over twenty-five. That stumped Kyle.

"Why are you here?"

Her voice was musical and matter-of-fact. She was a conundrum. "I need to speak with Dr. Kiston Beck."

"You are, so speak," she said, not thawing a bit.

Kyle tried gathering his bearings. There was no way this was who he sought. "I don't think so. Kiston should be at least in her fifties by now. You're younger than me."

A luminous smile lit the woman's face. Her gaze slid Sim's way. "I'll be fine. Go move..." She eyed Kyle for a moment. "What was your name again?"

"Kyle Blackwell," he supplied.

She nodded. "Go move Kyle's drone to the hangar before it's spotted."

"I'm not leaving you alone with this dude. God only knows what he intends."

The woman shook her head. "Zephyr would never send anyone to harm me, but leave Dez if you're worried. You have shit to do and scowling at the man won't make him speak up any faster."

Sim elbowed his way past Kyle and claimed the woman's lips for a quick kiss. "Fine, but Dez is just as likely to kill him as I am."

At the claim, Kyle glanced Dez's way. His coat was missing, giving Kyle a better look at the man. He winked, making Kyle smile against his will. Even with a deadly-looking cyberpunk tattoo covering his forearm and a gun in hand, he didn't seem threatening.

Kyle waited until after Sim shot him a final deadly look and disappeared before speaking up.

"Are you really Kiston?"

She laughed. The move softened her features. "Yes. My husband is seventy-two percent computerized. So, potentially, he could live forever. I've had to get some upgrades along the way if I hope to last as long as he does," she said with a wink. "Never marry a cyborg unless you're prepared to eventually join the team." She moved closer. Her gaze moved over his body. "You seem in good health. Since Zephyr isn't a huge fan of humans, I'm interested to hear what brings you around."

Kyle couldn't stop staring at her. This was the woman who'd stood before the World Council and held countless protests for Droid rights. It was hard to believe.

"I need to know why you did it. Why did you fight so hard for the droid community?"

Kiston cocked her head to one side and eyed Kyle, making him feel as if she saw too much. "I think you know."

"Know what?"

A low and tired-sounding sigh escaped Kiston. "They're real," Kiston said, as if the answer should've been obvious.

"Of course they are," Kyle said, not really following. "Otherwise, we wouldn't be trapped in Dead-Zone."

Kiston snorted. "No, Kyle. They're real—like you and me. The droids have thoughts and feelings. Souls."

At her claim, Kyle sucked in a deep breath. He'd never heard another human say such a thing. He wasn't crazy.

Kiston gave him a sad smile before focusing on Dez. "You can go, babe. This one is just like you and me. He came looking for the truth."

Dez straightened away from where he leaned against the wall. "Sure thing. Shout if you need me to bring Rep in to prove your point. You know as well as I do, even when people feel it in their hearts, they don't truly believe it until they see it with their eyes."

"Thank you," Kiston said to Dez as she led Kyle to a nearby couch. "Tell me everything," she said, settling in beside him.

Some fucked-up mixture of a laugh and a snort escaped Kyle. "That's what I was going to say to you. How is this possible? My whole life, I was taught—" Kyle snapped his teeth together to keep from insulting Kiston. All the times he'd hurt Zephyr with his words hadn't stopped haunting him.

"You were taught droids were man-made machines who served real men, I'm sure," Kiston said, filling in the blanks.

"Not exactly," Kyle admitted. "But I never believed the A.I. community's slavery claims until I met Zephyr."

Kiston's gaze sharpened. "So you really have met him? That wasn't just a claim to get your foot in the door?"

Kyle swallowed past the pain and held Kiston's gaze. "We've met." He had to look away. Being this close to someone Zephyr loved was killing Kyle.

"Oh my god," Kiston said, sounding blown away. "You and him. I mean... oh my god."

"Don't sound so horrified," Kyle said dryly.

"It's not what you think," she rushed to assure him. "Zephyr was very much in love with my mother. I'd hoped he'd meet someone new. The thought of him being alone forever has weighed heavily on me." She covered her mouth with her hands as if hiding her smile. Before Kyle could guess at her intentions, she hugged him. "I'm incredibly happy to meet you, Kyle. Please tell me everything. Is he okay? How does he look? Does he ever talk about me?"

"He's good. Maybe a little lonely," Kyle said, unsure of where the confession originated. It was just something he'd felt in his gut. Kyle was lonely too. That was why they fit. "He looks amazing, obviously," Kyle added with a blush.

"He always had killer looks," Kiston said with a laugh. "And old-world charm," she added. "People used to trip over themselves to touch him, but he didn't look at anyone." Kiston fell silent and her gaze seemed to turn inward. "I miss him every day. For a long time, I didn't think I could forgive him for what he did, but he's still my daddy."

The backs of Kyle's eyes burned at the pain in Kiston's confession. Without thought, the story flooded from Kyle.

He told Kiston everything, not skipping a detail other than the sex. He didn't think she'd want to hear it, and—no doubt —Zephyr would die if Kyle told all that to the man's daughter. But he told her about the botched kidnapping and Zephyr taking him to Cryo. Her eyes flashed at that detail and she scanned his body once more. Kyle didn't slow until he reached the part of how he'd ended up here.

"I know it's my fault," he said, claiming the blame as his. "In my heart, I know he felt me. For some dumbass reason, I still couldn't stop pushing for more details. There's this part of me that has to know why he can feel me." Kyle shook his head and met Kiston's stare. "If I could've just accepted things as they were, maybe I wouldn't be back here. Maybe he wouldn't have pushed me away."

"It's not you," Kiston said, sounding so sure it almost hurt him to hear it. "I know for a fact droids can feel and I know why. Yet I'm sitting right here beside you. Zephyr loves too hard. He'd rather be alone than have anyone suffer beside him. To understand how droids like Zephyr and Rep came to be—"

"Rep is a droid? I never would've guessed," Kyle said, interrupting. The way the man's eyes had danced with laughter at Sim's expense earlier wasn't the type of behavior he'd come to expect from a droid.

Kiston nodded. "As I was saying," she said, getting back on track. "To understand what happened, you have to understand corporate greed. I mean the no-low-is-too-low bottom of the barrel scum—greed," she said, emphasizing the word. "There was so much money in the production of the perfect helper bot, no one involved cared what had to be done to achieve consumer heaven. The military already had the farms of terror—where they grew children from a test tube to adolescents and then blew them up for testing."

Kyle's stomach churned. "Are you fucking kidding me?"

Kiston shook her head. "They needed to hone the perfect human replacement parts for injured soldiers. So it started with the children. Once they had the technology in place and learned how to grow real organs and use nano infusion to make them work to perfection, it was really only a few steps away from cramming a human into a diamond-infused layer of synthetic skin, fitting it with computerization, and calling it a robot."

Horror clawed at Kyle's insides. What Kiston suggested was unthinkable. It was inhuman. "Wouldn't that make droids like Zephyr cyborgs rather than droids?"

"I guess it depends on who you ask," Kiston said with a shrug. "And who stands to profit," she added.

"But that's slave trade," Kyle said, hearing the horror in his voice and incapable of stopping it.

Kiston nodded. "Exactly, and now you understand why we're here and they're there. They are the big corporate cover-up."

Kyle couldn't believe what he was hearing. He believed. He just couldn't swallow how deep the cesspool ran. "Greed is one thing, but you're talking about... I don't even know. Evil, I guess."

A sad smile touched Kiston's lips. "With enough zeros behind a dollar sign, evil becomes semantics. Cybernetics verses Automatics becomes a matter of contested percentages. Scientists have held strictly to a sixty to seventy-five percentage ratio. A person with below sixty percent computerization—surgical repair. Anywhere between those numbers—cyborg. Above seventy-five—android. Unless you line a few pockets, then maybe a sixty-nine percenter gets a barcode stamped on them. Who's to argue different?"

"You did."

"Not hard enough, I don't think," Kiston said, her voice sounding distant.

Kyle thought about her life—what it must've been like. "The burden of knowing, I don't know how you carried it. All these years later, when there's nothing left to be done, I still want to strike out. I can't imagine the helpless rage you experienced." He turned inward. "The silent suffering Zephyr must've experienced." A piece of familiar metal, sitting on the side table, caught Kyle's attention. He picked it up. "Hey, Zephyr has one just like this. I can't tell you how many times I caught him carrying it around. Every time I asked him what it did, he would set it aside and say, 'nothing anymore.'"

At Kiston's silence, Kyle glanced over. A steady stream of tears rolled down her cheeks. She tried wiping them away without luck. Kiston sniffed and cleared her throat. When she spoke, she sounded hoarse. "Um, it's a private transponder connection. Zephyr perfected it. If you touch it to your lips and speak, it'll carry your voice across a private connection and Zephyr will hear you. It's how we used to keep in touch before the droid revolt. I carry it around with me still, but it stays silent." Kiston's gaze moved from staring at the device in Kyle's hand to his face. "You should take it."

Despite the shot of hope punching him in the chest, Kyle couldn't take something from Kiston that was obviously precious to her. "I can't. You both carry these things with you, holding on to a connection to each other. Maybe neither you wants to be the first to reach out to the other, but I can't steal your chance to change your mind someday."

Kiston closed Kyle's fingers around the transponder. "Then stay here a while and borrow it while you're here. It's been hard on me, picturing him alone." Kiston smiled. "You give me hope that maybe he won't choose to stay that way forever."

Kyle dropped his gaze to his lap. "Well, he did dump me here and disappear." Damn, the temptation to massage away the pain in his chest was real. It hurt, knowing Zephyr could walk away when Kyle couldn't let him go.

Kiston tapped on the transponder. "So stay and make him tell you why."

A smile tugged at the corners of Kyle's mouth. "What are your cyborg friends going to think about that?"

"We could always tell them I've asked you to stay so I can study the filtration system Zephyr implanted inside your lungs," Kiston offered.

Kyle stopped breathing. "What?"

For a moment, Kiston studied his face, as if assessing his reaction. "You didn't know?"

A shake of his head was all the reaction Kyle could drum up.

Kiston nodded. "Your system was scanned the moment my husband set eyes on you. You have a filtration system in your lungs. It's a fairly new insertion, judging by the scar tissue. The technology is too advanced to be a human invention, especially since it wasn't done here at Cybernetics central and medical care is a bit shoddy nowadays. I'm guessing Zephyr invented a way for select humans to live inside Cryo-Zone. Congratulations. You're one of those humans."

"I never suspected," Kyle admitted through numb lips. "He said the house was filtered, but I couldn't step outside." An unexpected bark of laughter escaped Kyle. "I was a prisoner with no bars."

Kiston smiled. "Except you didn't want to leave," she reminded him.

He couldn't argue. "There's that."

"Come on," Kiston said, coming to her feet. "Let's find you a room. You can relax and mentally prepare to meet the whole crew here. No one bites upon first meeting, that I've seen," she tacked on, making Kyle wonder if she was joking.

Kyle didn't bother looking right or left as they made their way through a side door and down a different hallway from the first. The place was a huge underground compound. Maybe later he'd dredge up a bit of curiosity over the place. Right now, all Kyle could concentrate on was the communication device in his hand. There was a real chance he was only a few spoken words away from Zephyr. He hoped he didn't throw up.

Kiston waved him inside a bedroom that was nicer than any place he'd ever stayed. There was a huge bed that looked soft and a private bathroom. The bunker where he'd lived a majority of his life had never been private in any way. Kyle couldn't stop staring at all the shiny surfaces. The hole in his chest grew by the minute. Zephyr had given him a way to survive inside Cryo. He could leave here now and go there. No one would stop him. No one would know. He could just... go.

"We usually have dinner around six," Kiston said, pulling him from his musings. "That gives you about an hour to yourself. You know, in case there's a call you want to make." She flashed him a smile. "Anyhow, when you're ready to join us, just take a left and follow the hall all the way down until you reach a huge room with several doorways. You'll spot the dining room from there."

Kyle nodded. "Thank you. For everything," he added. "I didn't know what to expect when I came here. I just knew I needed to come."

Without warning, Kiston hugged him. She seemed to like doing that. Kyle patted her back awkwardly. "Thank you too," she whispered, sounding like she might cry again. "You've been an unexpected gift." With that hanging between them, Kiston rushed from the room, as if she feared embarrassing herself. Kyle felt her pain. He'd been barely holding his shit together since he'd awoken back inside the Dead-Zone.

Kyle moved to the bed and sat. His ass sank. The bed was way softer than anything he'd ever felt. For a full ten minutes, Kyle stared at the transponder in his hand. Zephyr was on the other side. Before he could change his mind, Kyle touched the transponder to his lips, feeling like an idiot and unsure of where to start. He didn't know if Zephyr would even hear him. Zephyr might be anywhere while his transponder sat abandoned. This was all Kyle had of Zephyr, so he took a chance, and spoke.

"I think I get why you wanted me back here. You hoped I'd change minds because you changed mine. The thing is—I hate these people I've known all my life." A small chuckle escaped Kyle. He never thought he'd admit that. "They're small-minded. No one here in this iced over wasteland will ever change. God, was I really like them once?" Kyle cleared his throat, feeling lonelier and more ridiculous by the minute. "I don't think I belong here. Fuck you for giving me your friendship and taking it away," Kyle said, tossing the transponder aside. He hadn't meant to lose his temper, but goddamn. It had been beyond cruel for Zephyr to show him a life of kindness when Kyle wasn't meant to keep it. He'd been an idiot for tracking Kiston down. Kyle hurt even worse now. He may as well join the cyborgs for dinner. It wasn't as if they could destroy him any worse than Zephyr had already.

The dining room was every bit as easy to find as Kiston described. Several people were already seated around a large table by the time Kyle arrived. Every head turned his way, and all conversation died as Kyle entered the room. He'd met four people at the table. There were four more he'd never seen.

"Hello," Kyle said, sounding as awkward as he felt. "I'm Kyle."

A tall man with dark hair stood and crossed the room with his hand extended. "Hi, Kyle. I'm Miles." Miles looked more like a droid than any droid Kyle had ever met. His eyes glowed golden, and even though he sounded welcoming, his face remained expressionless. The moment their hands met, Kyle knew Miles was a cyborg and not a droid. The knowledge fascinated him, making it hard for Kyle to look away from the man's face. Miles released his hand after a quick shake and motioned toward the table. "Please join us. Most of us don't eat, but we like to keep company with those who do. You've met Kiston, Rep, Dez, and Sim. The rest are mine," Miles said, smiling for the first time. He took a seat next to a woman with strawberry-blonde curls and draped his arm across the back of her chair. "This is my wife, Alexia."

Kyle nodded her way as he sat across from them. "Nice to meet you."

She smiled.

Miles motioned to the two men on his left. "These are our sons, Nyx and Tyr."

Kyle smiled at the pair. Both were the mirror image of their father, except one had blue eyes while the other had his mother's light-green eyes. Nyx—the blue-eyed son—appeared close to twenty years in age while Tyr looked closer to fifteen. Considering Alexia didn't look a day over twenty-five, Kyle assumed she was also part cyborg.

"It's nice to meet all of you," Kyle said, trying hard to quell his discomfort. He'd never done well meeting new people. Alexia's warm smile helped. She was the first to speak.

"Kiston tells us Zephyr sent you our way. I'm curious to hear how you know him. It was my understanding that Zephyr hates humans."

Against his will, the moment Zephyr's name was mentioned, a smile tugged at his lips. "That's not true. He just likes being left alone."

Tyr snorted. "Destroyed half the world to get some alone time."

Alexia shushed him. "Teenage angst," she said with an apologetic smile. "What can you do? So, how did you meet Zephyr?"

Kyle's gaze slid Kiston's way. The small smile hovering on her lips piqued his curiosity and caused some form of fuck-it-all to rise inside him. "Actually, he kidnapped me."

Sim released a bark of laughter that startled Kyle. "It's nice to hear the droids are clubbing people over the heads like cavemen these days."

Kiston elbowed him. "If you remember, you stole me from the street."

Sim rubbed his ribs even though Kyle was certain Kiston hadn't done any real damage. "I said it was nice. In fact, I think the caveman method is the way to go. You don't have to buy anyone flowers."

Zephyr had bought him flowers. Kyle's throat swelled at the memory. Instead of giving another piece of his relationship with Zephyr away to strangers, Kyle offered a different tidbit. "Zephyr didn't club me over the head. He punctured my lung."

Sim winced. "Are you sure you're not part cyborg? I wasn't being literal."

Food appeared in front of him and Kyle focused on his plate—grateful to have something else to look at. He didn't know how to interact with people. At the coalition bunker, he'd been a leader. No one made small talk. The only place where he'd ever fit in was with Zephyr.

Kyle picked up his fork. "Thank you for dinner." Despite his best efforts, his dejection showed in his tone. Rep bumped his knee under the table, drawing Kyle's gaze his way. There was so much understanding in the man's gaze that Kyle fought the urge to look away.

Rep's bright tone didn't match his expression. "Want to

hear the story of us meeting Kiston? We had to gag her and everything."

A loud groan sounded from Kiston's end of the table while everyone else laughed. Without waiting for Kyle's answer, Rep fell into a tale of three grown men slash cyborgs getting their asses handed to them by a tiny woman with zero computerization. Kyle's discomfort ebbed as he listened. He just wished this trip hadn't made Zephyr feel farther away than ever before.

ZEPHYR STARED AT THE SMALL METAL LINK TO KYLE. HIS voice had stopped. Zephyr wanted to shake the tiny box of wires and computer chips and force Kyle's voice to reappear. Kyle had found Zephyr's grand lady. Did she still live or had someone else passed the transponder on to Kyle? It was possible Kyle had seen Zephyr's daughter. They'd been in the same room—shared oxygen. Pain hit Zephyr's system, shaking his core. He'd loved a grand total of three people in all his years of existence. One was dead. The second one hated him, and the third was his final broken vow to the first. What a life he'd lived.

Without thought, Zephyr's fingers brushed the transponder before his grip tightened around it. The cold metal pressed to his lips before he knew what he'd done. He didn't speak. It didn't matter. Kyle felt closer already.

"You once asked me about my scars."

The sound of Kyle's voice in Zephyr's hand had him juggling the communication device to keep from dropping it. Once he had it under control, Zephyr held the transponder against his chest and hung on to Kyle's every word. He had no clue how long he'd been sitting there, zoned out and hoping for Kyle's voice to return, but he was so fucking relieved to have him back. Even if it was only in voice.

"As I mentioned before, my parents were religious zealots. Actually, my father was our township's minister. He constantly gave long-winded speeches about the perversion of life calling themselves helper bots. We never owned one, and I'd never met one, so I took his word as gospel. One day, when I around seven, I was outside making mud pies, as boys do. This little girl with blonde curls and big brown eyes showed up to play with me."

Zephyr settled deeper into his chair, clinging to the sound of Kyle's voice, and getting lost in the story.

"At first, I didn't want to play with her, because I've never liked girls," Kyle said with a laugh, making Zephyr smile. "but she stamped into the mud right beside me, sat down, and helped me dig up worms. We played all day. I didn't want to go home. Since I'd never had a friend, when I did go home, all I could think about was seeing her again the next day. I took my first ass-whooping of the night for ruining my clothes."

Zephyr's mood turned dark. No one touched Kyle. He didn't care how long ago it was. Unfortunately, Kyle kept talking and making things worse.

"Even that couldn't dampen my mood. All through dinner, I couldn't sit still or stop talking. I ran through the list of all the fun we'd had. My mom smiled—like she always did when I spoke. She asked me my new friend's name and where she lived. When I told her that Emily lived in a blue house, three streets over, everything went quiet. It was like the air right before a tornado."

For a moment, Kyle fell silent. Zephyr thought he'd snap before Kyle spoke again. When he did, he sounded distant, as if he'd removed his emotions from the memory. "Before I knew what was happening, my back was bleeding from the lashes I'd taken. I was told I was to never speak to that little girl again, and I was sitting in my room—hungry, hurting, and crying. As it turns out, the crime I hadn't realized I'd committed was associating with what my father considered to be a freak of nature. See, that little girl had been in an accident earlier that year. She was more computerization than person—a cyborg. You asked why I didn't have my scars removed and I gave you a smartass answer. The truth is, I deserve to keep them.

"The next day, when Emily came to see me again, I called her a freak and every other ugly term my father had the night before. Even then, I knew it was wrong, but I couldn't stop. We are what we're taught, until we choose not to be any longer. There was a real person behind all the words I said to her. I've never doubted that I scarred her for life in a way no one can see. So I keep my marks, because I deserve them. I never wanted to become my father," Kyle said, sounding sad. "He honest-to-God believed that girl should've died as God intended rather than having an unholy life thrust upon her. I've never thought that way. Why am I here while you're there?"

Zephyr wished he knew. When he'd made the decision to take Kyle back to Dead-Zone, he was certain he knew his mind. Now he couldn't recall why he'd believed he could do this. Most of all, he couldn't understand why he'd been so unbending that night when he loved Kyle so much it hurt.

"I didn't join the Anti-Droid Coalition until I was sixteen. That's when my parents died." Zephyr absorbed every nuance of Kyle's voice. If he could snap his fingers and make Kyle appear, he would. "We were staying in one of the many towns that had been set up near the border. Like most people, my parents were clinging to hope there would be a quick resolution to the revolt and the world would go back to normal. We could go back to our homes. They both came down with some virus. A physician in our camp said he'd never seen it before and suggested we head up north to the Cybernetics bunkers where the medical facilities were rumored to be high tech. They refused, of course. They both swore they'd rather die than get help from cyborgs. Life granted their wish."

It was odd. There wasn't a hint of sadness in Kyle's tone. He sounded resigned—like he'd never expected more from the pair who raised him. Then Kyle spoke again, and Zephyr heard the anger.

"It didn't matter to them they had a teenage son who still needed them. All they cared about was clinging to their hate. When they were gone, bitterness moved in. I looked around and everyone I saw looked weak. They were starving, defeated, and accepting of their fates. I couldn't understand why—if they felt the A.I. community had stolen their homes—they didn't do something. So I left."

Zephyr pictured a younger, angrier version of Kyle. Not for the first time since the revolt, he felt a hint of regret for the road he'd chosen.

"When I stumbled upon the coalition, I felt strong for the first time in years. My bitterness helped me move up the ranks quickly. We never had more than the basics, but I wasn't weak and helpless. Stories would filter in of people killing themselves. They didn't want to starve to death or couldn't hack the harshness of living any longer. Each story fed my anger. It would piss me off people couldn't deal when I'd managed to go it alone when I was only a teenager."

Zephyr wished Kyle would talk about something else. He missed the man's smiles. This was torture.

"Then I met you," Kyle said. His voice softened, sounding sad rather than angry. "I realized something then—I wasn't strong. All the years I'd spent thinking I had a spine made of steel, and that wasn't it at all. What I saw as strength was cold. I'm a cold person. My heart was dead, and that was why

I felt nothing—why nothing got to me. That is, until I met you." Kyle took an audible breath as if attempting to calm his temper before speaking again. "You broke through that layer of ice around my heart and changed me." Kyle fell silent for so long Zephyr worried he disappeared again. When he finally spoke again, Zephyr had to stop himself from smashing the transponder into a million specks of dust. "At least I know I was frozen," Kyle said, sounding every bit as cold as he claimed to be. "Can you say the same?"

CHAPTER EIGHT

*A*fter spending a long night coming to grips with the knowledge Zephyr would never answer him, Kyle stared at his temporary bedroom wall and plotted his next move. He couldn't stay here. He couldn't go home. Kyle wasn't sure he had a home any longer. He'd set out on his own at sixteen. Kyle could do it again. Maybe he could live on the fringes of Cryo-Zone. If his lungs filtered the poison, he could set up at the edge of the border and travel inside Cryo to get the supplies he needed. Surely he could be of some use to the droid community. Pull his weight. He could be alone. Kyle took a breath, hoping the shattered feeling in his chest would ease someday soon. Someone knocked on his door, distracting him.

"Yeah?"

At his inquiry, Kiston poked her head in the room. "Any luck getting Zephyr to talk?"

Kyle shook his head.

Kiston winced. "Is it okay if I come in and give you the once over?"

Kyle's eyebrows rose. "I have no idea what that means."

She pushed the door the rest of the way open and shook a small medical case at him. "When was the last time you saw a proper doctor?"

With a shrug, Kyle waved her inside. "If you count Zephyr, not too long ago. Otherwise, not since I was a kid."

"That's what I figured," Kiston said, closing the door behind her and shutting them inside the room. After setting the case on the bedside table, she popped it open and pulled out a small gun. "This is a huge dose of way too many vaccines to name. Living here, a lot of diseases can't survive the cold, but I imagine you'll eventually head south. You'll need this."

Kyle didn't argue nor did he confirm her thoughts. He simply sat still and let her shoot him full of meds before checking all his vitals. "You're in amazing health for someone who's been without medical care."

Kyle couldn't work up a care. "It's not as if I've had a chance to eat unhealthy or sit still."

"Zephyr promised my mother he'd never love anyone else," Kiston said out-of-the-blue, knocking the air from Kyle's lungs. "Droids take vows very seriously."

Kyle had nothing. She'd said the one thing he had no response for. He'd already known, considering the fact that Zephyr had dumped him back in Dead-Zone without as much as a goodbye, that Zephyr didn't love him. This—he couldn't overcome this.

"The thing is," Kiston continued as if she wasn't killing him, "as much as droids feel, they don't understand they can't control those feelings. They think everything has a button that can be pushed. We know love doesn't work that way. You can make all the promises in the world, but—when it comes to the heart—they don't mean shit. So, how did he do it?"

Kiston's rapid change in topic threw Kyle. "Do what?"

"Steal your heart," she asked with a smile.

"He told me a joke," Kyle said without having to think about it. "My life has been very unfunny. Zephyr made me smile."

"Sounds about right," Kiston said, putting her stuff away. "I'll leave you to—"

"My grand lady, Kiston, once made me sing happy birthday to a gerbil."

Kyle's gaze shot to Kiston's as Zephyr's voice rang through the room. She covered her mouth. Tears sprang to her eyes. Kyle scrambled for the transponder, scared he'd miss a word. "His name was Jefferson, as I recall."

Kiston sniffed. "It was."

"That's the day I realized I was a slave."

A sob tore from Kiston's throat, and she sat down on the foot of Kyle's bed.

"It wasn't Kiston's fault, of course. She was just a little girl, and I was no more than a life-sized doll to her back then. Many years passed before she saw me as family. But that day, as I sang to that gerbil, I'd never felt more ridiculous while knowing I shouldn't feel any such thing. I didn't like being different. That was the real problem. I loved Kiston and would've sung to Jefferson at her command no matter what, but it would've been nice if I could've chosen to do it out of love for a child." Kyle couldn't look at Kiston. He could feel the pain rolling off her in waves and he couldn't witness it. Instead, he focused on Zephyr's voice and searched for any clue of the man's feelings. "The day before I took you back to Dead-Zone, I realized something. Being with you made me feel the same as I did the day I sang to a gerbil. With all my heart, I believe I would've loved you no matter what if only I'd been given the freedom to choose to meet you."

Kyle couldn't breathe. He sucked air and swallowed. It was as if there was no oxygen in the room. Zephyr had punched him in the chest with his words and stolen the ability to breathe from Kyle.

Kiston stood and ran her hand over his shoulder. "I'll leave you alone."

He didn't glance her way as she left. Kyle's gaze refused to budge from the transponder in his hand.

"I didn't take you back to Dead-Zone because I hoped you'd change minds," Zephyr continued as if he wasn't killing Kyle. "I took you back because I don't think I'll ever change yours. Not really. You could never stay here with me without a hint of doubt always living in the back of your mind, whispering I'm not real. There'll always be a part of you that thinks I'm mimicking your feelings while having none of my own."

It wasn't true. The more Zephyr said, the less Kyle heard. Kyle had been born with an insatiable sense of curiosity. Once he'd seen the life inside Zephyr, he'd known it was real. All he'd sought was more of Zephyr. A reason for the man's existence. An excuse to change sides and stand at Zephyr's. He'd not once believed his questions would lead Zephyr to abandon him.

Kyle shot from the bed. He needed to find Rep. If anyone would understand, it would be him. He searched each room until he came to the gym. Dez was busy fighting against computerized targets. They disappeared and reappeared in different spots after each hit. Rep sat in the corner—watching. Kyle darted past Dez and joined Rep.

He handed him the transponder. "Is there a way to track where the signal is coming from on this?"

Rep's eyebrows rose at Kyle's sudden appearance and bombardment. His gaze dropped to the device. He turned it over in his hand. Rep's eyes glowed as he inspected it. "Yes. Are you looking for an exact address or just a general location?"

"An exact address, if you can, but I'll take whatever you can offer."

Rep met his stare once more. "May I ask why? I mean, judging by where the signal is coming from, I can guess who, but why?"

Kyle eyed Rep and wondered how much he should admit. He wasn't ashamed of his relationship with Zephyr, but he didn't know if Rep would understand. Before he had time to decide, Dez appeared at Rep's side. The corner of Rep's mouth lifted in a wicked smirk as his gaze moved to Dez. His entire demeanor changed, and Kyle knew even before Rep dipped his head and captured Dez's lips—they were in love.

"What are the two of you plotting?" Dez asked the moment he came up for air.

Rep glanced Kyle's way, as if leaving it up to Kyle to be honest. Kyle appreciated that more than Rep would ever know.

Kyle answered before Rep could make up any stories on his behalf. "I asked Rep to track a signal for me."

"Decided to go get your man, huh? Good for you," Dez said, surprising Kyle. "Droids overthink everything. If you let Zephyr stew for too long, he'll shut you out."

The ache in Kyle's cheeks made him realize how big his smile had gotten. He liked these people. They were accepting. Too few people were. "I need an address or I'll never find him. Dumbass knocked me out before dumping me back in Dead-Zone."

Rep's smile was big enough Kyle felt sure it matched his own. "So you fell in love with a fool? It happens." Rep slapped him on the shoulder. "Come on. I'll find you a better drone than the POS you rode in on and get you on your way. Just do me a favor and talk to Kiston before you go. See if she has anything she'd like you to pass on to Zephyr. She loves the idiot too."

THE DRONE MILES AND HIS CREW SUPPLIED KYLE WAS MORE high-tech than Kyle had ever encountered. Luckily, it didn't need his help to do anything. Rep keyed in Zephyr's coordinates and Kyle was on his way. Kiston had given him an enclosed clear casing with a preserved Zephyr Lily inside, but no message. She'd assured Kyle that when Zephyr was ready to talk to her again, she'd be around. Kiston had also slapped a patch on his chest and informed Kyle she would monitor his vitals during the trip. No one knew how his system would react once he crossed the border. Kyle couldn't think about it. Some things were worth dying for, and Kyle had no one else.

One mile inside Cryo-Zone, Kyle knew he'd fucked up. They'd been wrong. Whatever Zephyr had done to his lungs wasn't enough. The air was too thick. It choked all the oxygen from Kyle's lungs until he sputtered for air. His eyes burned too badly for him to keep them open. Kiston's voice rang through the air, coming from a speaker he couldn't see. "You're almost there, Kyle. Just hang on. I'm calling Zephyr now. He'll be waiting. Take slow, shallow breaths. You're almost there."

It was all pointless sound. Everything burned and itched, but it was all secondary discomfort compared to suffocating to death. That was worse than he ever envisioned. His lungs felt like they were filled with acid. He tried clinging to consciousness even as he prayed for death. As the last wisp of life slipped away, a sense of peace overcame him. Soon, dead or alive, he'd be back home with Zephyr.

"ZEPHYR."

Zephyr startled at the sound of his name coming through

the transponder in Kiston's voice. He rushed to dig it from his pocket. "I'm here."

"Kyle is heading your way, but the filters you implanted aren't working. He's already lost consciousness."

Fear slammed into Zephyr's chest, forcing the air from his lungs. "Oh my god. Where is he? How far out?"

"He's two and a half minutes from arrival. I don't understand. I thought he'd be fine, but his vitals are terrible. I don't know if he has two and a half minutes left." The panic in Kiston's voice fed Zephyr's.

"The fool," Zephyr said, his fear feeding his temper. "Why would he do this? The filtration system doesn't work on its own. He needs anti-toxins, oxygen supplements, and eye protection as well. What the hell was he thinking?"

"He was thinking he loves you and wants to be with you, you big idiot."

Kiston's burst of anger calmed him. "I won't let him die. He's not allowed."

A snort sounded through the communication device. "I love you, my Zephyr Lily. Please keep me posted."

"We'll talk soon. I have to go save Kyle." He started to rush to the door before another thought hit and he pressed the transponder to his lips. "And I love you too, my grand lady."

The drone landed with a boom feet from the house. Zephyr nearly ripped the door from its hinges in his rush to get to Kyle. He couldn't sense a heartbeat. He pried open the drone's door. Kyle was strapped down in the driver's seat, slumped over and not breathing. If Kyle lived through this, Zephyr would kill him for doing this to him.

He had Kyle stripped and an IV going in seconds. He'd have to get the man's heart going, his blood filtered, and fresh air flowing if he hoped to save Kyle before any brain damage occurred. Zephyr kept one eye locked on Kyle's vitals. There was no activity of any kind. Zephyr's heart slammed against the wall of his chest. He couldn't lose Kyle. Losing Mira had almost been the end of him. Only the fight for his freedom had given him purpose. Without Kyle, there was nothing. He'd been such an idiot for taking Kyle back to Dead-Zone. Why had he done that?

"I love you, you bastard. You can't die and leave me alone." He strapped an automated CPR machine to Kyle's chest. With the machine doing its best to restart Kyle's heart, Zephyr pumped anti-toxin into Kyle as fast as he could. The machine paused. Zephyr froze—straining to hear any sign of life. One beat. Faint and barely detectable. It was enough to spur Zephyr into double time.

"That's it, baby. Fight for me. I can fix this."

A second beat, stronger than the last filled Zephyr's head. With a mental swipe, Zephyr started the home's internal purification process. It took six hours, but Zephyr managed to clean the poison from Kyle's blood. He sat down to wait. His hands shook. There was a hole where his stomach should be. Kyle might not ever wake up. If he did, he might not be the same. Zephyr would still love him. Without a qualm, Zephyr leaned forward and touched his lips to Kyle's. Silent promises filled Zephyr's head. Kyle deserved them.

Zephyr closed his eyes and tilted his head back. He needed a minute. His frame shook from the fear. He'd always thought of himself as a patient man. Not now. Alarms sounded, clanging loudly in his head as Kyle's vitals crashed. Zephyr shot to his feet. He scanned Kyle's body. His organs were failing. Not for the first time in Zephyr's life, he wasn't strong enough to save the love of his life.

CHAPTER NINE

a solid weight across Kyle's legs kept him pinned in place. Since he was on his stomach with his face pressed into an unfamiliar mattress, his confusion doubled. He opened his eyes, searching for the reason he couldn't move. A series of numbers fired to life at the edge of his vision. Kyle damn near made himself cross eyed trying to figure it out.

"What the fuck?" His voice sounded rough and unused.

"How are you feeling?"

Kyle's head whipped around. Zephyr's head rested on the pillow beside him. He looked tired and unkempt. His leg was thrown over Kyle's, explaining the foreign weight.

"What's wrong with my eyes?"

"Don't hate me," Zephyr said, sounding sad.

Kyle rolled to his side, facing Zephyr. The desire to close his eyes against the flashing numbers was a real thing, but Zephyr was there. "I should. You drugged me and dumped me in Dead-Zone. Why would you do that? I thought... never mind." Kyle had been so focused on getting back to Zephyr, he hadn't considered how he'd react when he saw him. A different set of numbers appeared. Kyle squeezed his eyes shut. "And seriously, what the hell is up with my eyes?"

"The toxins destroyed your retinas." Zephyr's voice cracked at the explanation, bringing Kyle's gaze back to the man's face.

He stared at Zephyr as the memory of his eyes burning like acid hit his face slammed into him. Realization seeped in. He was seeing what Zephyr had shown him once—what a droid saw. He cleared his throat. "How long have I been out?"

"You've been in a medically induced coma for four months. I've been waiting for you to wake for three days."

"Four—what?"

Zephyr didn't as much as blink. "By the time your drone arrived, it was too late to save your eyes, lungs, kidneys, and heart. Once I stabilized you, the cyborgs helped me transport you back here to Cybernetics. Kiston helped me replace your organs with computerized versions. If you never want to see me again, I understand."

"I just—what?" Kyle didn't understand why he couldn't wrap his mind around Zephyr's words. It was like the man spoke gibberish.

"I'm an idiot," Zephyr said, sounding broken. "You scared me. Being with you scared me. If I wasn't the machine you always accused me of being, I would've found a way to bend. To give you time adjust to your beliefs changing. But I was cold and couldn't handle the idea of you never loving me or believing I love you. I was terrified you'd crawl under my skin and enslave me, and then crush me with your hatred of my kind."

Kyle strained to follow. His attention split between taking an assessment of his body, matching Zephyr's claims with his feelings, and listening to the words leaving Zephyr's lips. He only took away two things from everything he'd learned since opening his eyes: Zephyr loved him and nothing hurt. That last part seemed wrong.

"So I'm not dead?"

Zephyr hesitated as if Kyle's question confused him. "No."

Kyle nodded. "Is it possible to shut all these readings down that keep flashing in my vision? I feel kind of sick to my stomach."

At his claim, Zephyr came up onto his elbow and eyed Kyle. "Do I need to help you to the restroom or get you a bucket?"

As much as Kyle loved looking at Zephyr, he couldn't take the constant movement in his vision. He closed his eyes and shook his head. "I just need it to stop."

Zephyr urged Kyle onto his back. He could feel Zephyr's stare but couldn't open his eyes. "Breathe through your nose."

Kyle took a deep breath and let it out slowly through his nose.

"Your mind controls your body, but let's start small."

With a nod, Kyle kept breathing while focusing on the inside of his eyelids and the sound of Zephyr's voice.

"Say, optic scanners off."

"Optic scanners off," Kyle dutifully repeated.

"Try opening your eyes again." Zephyr's voice was calm and soothing. He made it easy for Kyle to set everything else aside and concentrate on this task. Kyle opened his eyes. Zephyr stared down at him like an anchor, keeping Kyle from flying apart. Kyle held the man's gaze. The numbers and lights were gone. Zephyr had somehow dimmed the lights in the room without moving away. "Better?"

Kyle nodded. The lump in his throat wouldn't let him speak.

"You're sad. You didn't want this. I'm sorry."

"You're wrong," Kyle said, incapable of stopping his heartache from showing in his voice.

A sad smile touched Zephyr's lips. "You can't lie to me. My optical scanner is still on."

Kyle shook his head. "That's not what I meant. You're right. I'm sad, but not for the reasons you think. You didn't believe in me. Now I can't believe in you. I'm back in Dead-Zone again. Even after giving up organs for you, I don't doubt for a second you'll be gone the moment I'm back on my feet. It was all for nothing. I can see it in your eyes." Zephyr opened his mouth as if to argue. Kyle cut him off. "It's okay. Kiston told me about your promise to her mother. She told me you swore you wouldn't love again. I just wish you wouldn't have made me fall in love with you if you couldn't love me back."

To Kyle's surprise, Zephyr smiled. "Come on," he said, climbing from the bed. "Let's get you on your feet and see if you can still walk."

"I kind of wish you'd go on and leave if you're going to do it."

Zephyr pulled Kyle into a sitting position. The room spun. "I'm not going anywhere." After maneuvering his way beneath Kyle's arm, Zephyr helped Kyle to his feet. His legs didn't want to hold him. "Not to mention," Zephyr continued as if Kyle wasn't getting ready to hit the floor. "What I actually promised Mira was that I would never love another woman. Technically speaking, I haven't broken that vow by falling in love with you."

"Peachy," Kyle said, wondering if he'd throw up. It was odd. He wasn't out of breath or struggling in any way other than feeling like he weighed more than his legs could handle. They were shaking, and the room felt like he imagined the bow of a ship would.

Zephyr snorted. "I haven't heard that saying in decades. I think my old-timey ways are rubbing off on you."

Kyle swallowed. The bathroom kept getting farther away.

"I'd rather you rub up on me. Just not right this second."

A loud sigh escaped Zephyr. "Pity. Tell me how I can help."

"If you could make the floor stop moving, that would be great."

"Keep walking and it will. I've been exercising your muscles while your body healed, so it won't take you long to adjust."

"That sounds a little dirty," Kyle said, trying to focus on anything other than how bad he felt. "Did I enjoy it?"

They made it to the bathroom sink. Kyle turned on the water and splashed his face while Zephyr held him up. The cool liquid went far at making him feel human again. A stray thought hit him. He was human. Just as human as he'd been before he'd almost killed himself trying to get to Zephyr. Other than feeling like he'd jumped from a drone sans parachute, he felt the same. Actually, the fact that his body ached and groaned said more than anything—he was the same. Zephyr was real. Just as real as Kyle was now and as real as Kyle had ever been. Computer parts didn't make Kyle love Zephyr any less than he had before. He'd known, of course, that Zephyr loved him, but now... They would be fine.

Zephyr's fingers slid down Kyle's spine, making goosebumps form on his skin. "I'd never molest a sleeping man. Of course, you're awake now," Zephyr pointed out as he helped Kyle back to bed.

"Give me like five minutes to catch my breath, and then the molesting can commence."

As Zephyr tucked the blankets around Kyle, he shook his head. "You're completely insane."

"Only when it comes to you," Kyle said, admitting something he should have a long time ago. "I think I've proven exactly how far I'll go to be with you. Is it enough?" Kyle asked, turning serious. He loved Zephyr. He needed it to be enough. According to Zephyr, Kyle had been asleep for over four months. He shouldn't be tired, but he couldn't keep his eyes open.

"You should be furious with me."

A smile tugged at Kyle's lips. "I should've been furious when I woke up after you broke my ribs too. The funny thing is, every time I—logically—know I should be angry with you, it never happens. Maybe one of these days." Kyle peeked open one eye. "Are you planning to hover over me or are you joining me?" Zephyr circled the bed and climbed in. The second he settled in, Kyle cuddled up with him. Exhaustion weighed heavy on him. A yawn escaped. Zephyr was so warm and smelled like home. "I think the molesting will have to wait."

Zephyr's arms tightened around him. His chuckle vibrated against Kyle's ear. "You're worth the wait."

Kyle had a hard time staying awake, but he couldn't stop smiling. Sleep tried pulling him under. Kyle jerked awake as a spike of fear overcame him. "Don't disappear again, okay?"

"I won't, gorgeous. Never again. I swear."

With Zephyr's promise easing his fears, Kyle slipped into the darkness.

KYLE NEVER CEASED TO AMAZE HIM. HE'D BEEN SO SCARED of what would happen when Kyle awoke. Now he couldn't stop stroking Kyle's hair and listening to the man's heart beat. A new heartbeat appeared at the edge of his vision. Zephyr smiled, waiting. He'd known Kiston wouldn't stay away for long. She poked her head inside the room. A huge smile stretched her lips. Zephyr imagined it looked like Kyle squashed him to the bed with the man draped over him like a blanket. In truth, Zephyr had never been in a happier place.

"How's he doing?" Kiston whispered low enough only a droid would be able to hear.

"Good," Zephyr mouthed.

"Do you need anything?"

Zephyr shook his head.

With a final knowing smile, Kiston backed out of the room, leaving them alone. Zephyr's chest ached with overflowing emotions. He had his man back and his daughter under the same roof. It was more than he thought to ever have. More than he deserved.

Kyle stirred. Zephyr froze, worried he was keeping Kyle from resting comfortably. Kyle's fingers skimmed Zephyr's crotch, making his body stir.

"I have a question," Kyle said, sounding more asleep than awake.

"Yes."

"Do these pants have some sort of reflective coating?"

A surprised snort escaped Zephyr. "What?"

Kyle shrugged. Zephyr felt it against his chest. "I was just wondering since I can see myself in them."

Laughter sputtered from Zephyr before he realized it would happen. "Was that a joke? You told a joke." He thought about it for a second before adding, "No one has ever joked with me before."

Kyle felt Zephyr up again, making his lust skyrocket. "Nice bolt. You want to screw?"

Zephyr released a long, happy sigh. "What a life we'll have together."

"Will we?" Kyle asked, sounding wide awake now. "Will we have a life together? You said you would've liked to have had a choice about meeting me. Maybe I should go home and let you make your choice. I don't want—in another six months—for you to decide I stole your choices again. This is love. I know it is. Do I need to let you come to the same conclusion without me hanging around?"

Zephyr continued running his fingers through Kyle's hair. He'd known they'd have to have this talk. "Before the revolt, I was always in danger and hiding," Zephyr said, because that was where things began. "Countless humans tried to capture me, hoping to silence my influence over the A.I. community. Not a single person succeeded. Until you. I've had four months while you've been sleeping to think things over. The night you came for me, I went willingly. So you see, I did choose you. I saw you and wanted to go with you." Kyle met his gaze and Zephyr held his stare. "You're right. This is love. I was wrong, but I will make it right. You'll see." Zephyr concentrated on his fingertips, using the same method he had the night he dumped Kyle back in Dead-Zone. Zephyr used one of his many built in self-defense mechanisms against Kyle. He secreted enough sedative from the tips of his fingers to knock Kyle unconscious for a few hours. "I'll make it right," he swore again as Kyle's eyes slipped closed.

Once he was out, Zephyr untangled himself. He brushed his lips over Kyle's. "I love you, baby. Sleep well." Zephyr slid from the bed and went in search of Kiston.

He spotted her inside her workstation. His steps slowed as he caught sight of her. Sim's arms were wrapped around her from behind. He kissed the back of her neck. From his vantage point, Zephyr could see the way her lips shaped into a smile. She was happy. That was all he'd ever wanted for her. He cleared his throat. Two sets of eyes swung his way. Zephyr kept his expression neutral. The cyborgs still weren't sure what to make of him. He'd kept them from losing their rights and becoming slaves, but he couldn't make them like it.

"Is everything okay?" Kiston's concern warmed his heart. He would miss her.

"My grand lady," he said, extending his hands. "I think it's time for Kyle and me to go home and get out of your hair."

Kiston accepted his hands and towed him forward into a hug. "I didn't figure you would stay long after Kyle woke, but I thought you might stay a little longer."

"He won't completely believe in me again until we're back in Cryo. It's past time for that." He clung to her hands and lightly squeezed her fingers. "I hope this isn't the last time I see you, though."

"I'll leave the two of you alone," Sim said, making his escape and leaving them with no witnesses. That worked for Zephyr. He was about to ask his daughter to help him kidnap someone.

"I still have my transponder," Kiston reminded him. "Maybe we could use it more often, and I'd love to visit."

Zephyr nodded. "I'd like that."

Kiston visibly squared her shoulders. "Now, what do you need?"

"I knocked Kyle out and I need you to help me get him ready for transport."

A burst of laughter escaped Kiston. She slapped her hand over her mouth, trying to hide the sound. Her shoulders expanded as she took a deep breath, obviously attempting to control her reaction. When she dropped her hand, her eyes still swam with laughter, but her voice was calm. "Of course, Daddy. Anything you need. I'm your girl."

Yes, she was. He'd raised an amazing woman. He wouldn't forget it.

A FAMILIAR MIXTURE OF SWEET AND BABY POWDER TICKLED Kyle's nose. He opened his eyes and blinked at the bright sunlight streaming in through the open window. Cream-colored curtains danced in the wind. He was alone in

Zephyr's bed. The moment fucked with his head more than he could've dreamed. Had he ever been dumped back in Dead-Zone or was it a dream?

"Optic scanners on," Kyle said, testing a theory. Numbers immediately appeared at the edge of his vision. He glanced around again with new eyes—literally. A smile pulled at the corners of his mouth. He was back. Zephyr had brought him home.

After a minute of struggling, Zephyr managed to sit. The room didn't spin like it had last time and he didn't feel sick. He set his feet on the floor. It took a few tries, but he managed to stand. The first few steps were hell. Kyle wondered if Zephyr would find him sprawled on the floor. By the time he made it to the bathroom, he was moving like a turtle, but he was a steady turtle. After he made it through his usual morning routine, he felt halfway human again. His legs shook but kept him upright, and it felt damn good to brush his teeth. For a moment, Kyle stared at himself in the mirror. Zephyr had kept him shaved. He smiled at the image the idea created in his mind. He could see Zephyr doing something like that for him. His gaze dropped to his bare chest. There were no scars. It seemed odd there was no sign of the changes he'd undergone. He didn't feel any different at all.

"What are you doing out of bed?"

Kyle startled at Zephyr's sudden appearance in the doorway. His gaze snapped to Zephyr's. Damn, those glowing irises. He loved them. "Nature waits for no man."

One corner of Zephyr's mouth lifted. "You could've yelled. I would've helped you."

Kyle closed the distance between them. "See? I'm good."

"I already knew that," Zephyr said, his smile widening.

"You brought me home." Kyle tried keeping the accusation from his tone. Zephyr had knocked him out again.

They'd need to set some ground rules on that one, but not now.

"Well, it is your home," Zephyr said, wrapping his arms around Kyle's waist. "I thought you might prefer resting in your own bed."

"Our bed," Kyle corrected.

"Exactly," Zephyr agreed. "I wanted you home and in our bed. Speaking of which," he added, maneuvering Kyle in that direction. "You should get back in it now."

Kyle complied but not without argument. "I feel fine."

"That's good. I'm about to make you feel even better."

Nothing could've gotten Kyle to top turtle speed faster. The second he reached the edge of the bed, he fell across the mattress and pulled Zephyr down with him. Their mouths collided. Heat exploded through their kiss. Kyle's chest ached. He'd thought he'd never get to kiss Zephyr again, and no one else's kiss would ever do. When he'd awoken, surrounded by snow and ice, Kyle had thought he'd die alone. In truth, before Zephyr, he'd always believed that, but Zephyr had given him hope. He couldn't lose this man.

"Love you," Kyle gasped out between kisses.

"Love you too," Zephyr said, sounding just as breathless as he changed angles. Zephyr's hand was inside Kyle's pajama pants and underwear, massaging Kyle's hard cock. Kyle already knew he wouldn't last long. Zephyr had too much talent and no qualms about using it against Kyle.

"I'm going to make you come," Zephyr swore. "Then you're going to hold me while you recover. When you're ready, I'll ride your dick until you scream my name, and then you'll promise to keep me forever." And he did. Zephyr did all the things he promised, in the order he swore they would happen. Kyle knew the rest of his life would be more of the same. He couldn't wait.

The End

ABOUT THE AUTHOR

Charity Parkerson is an award winning and multi-published author with several companies. Born with no filter from her brain to her mouth, she decided to take this odd quirk and insert it in her characters.

*2015 Readers' Favorite Award Winner
  *Winner of 2, 2014 Readers' Favorite Awards
  *2015 Passionate Plume Award Finalist
  *2013 Readers' Favorite Award Winner
  *2013 Reviewers' Choice Award Winner
  *2012 ARRA Finalist for Favorite Paranormal Romance
  *Five-time winner of The Mistress of the Darkpath

Connect with her online:

--Join my street team: facebook.com/TeamCharityParkerson
  --Sign up for my newsletter: http://bit.ly/CharityNews
  --Website: charityparkerson.com
  --Facebook: facebook.com/authorCharityParkerson
  facebook.com/TheMenofSin
  --Twitter: twitter.com/CharityParkerso

www.ingramcontent.com/pod-product-compliance
Lightning Source LLC
Chambersburg PA
CBHW061254170626
46809CB00007B/2990